HUNTED

The Sierra Files, Book 2

By Christy Barritt

Hunted: A Novel
Copyright 2014 by Christy Barritt

Published by River Heights Press

Cover design by The Killion Group

The persons and events portrayed in this work are the
creation of the author, and any resemblance to persons
living or dead is purely coincidental.

CHAPTER 1

"So, Sierra, what do you think your parents' impression of me will be?" Chad asked.

I cringed as I weighed my response, trying to decide between brutal honesty and a vague resemblance of the truth. "I think they're going to be shocked."

He glanced at me, two hands still on the steering wheel of his faded orange, beach-certified vintage Vanagon. For his birthday, I'd even graced him with Hawaiian-inspired seat covers. I felt like a modern-day hippie whenever I rode in it.

"They'll be shocked?" Chad repeated, glancing over at me. "What's that mean? That they'll be shocked because I'm so good looking? Because they thought you'd be single forever? Because they won't think I'm your type?"

I cringed again. "Well . . . that, too."

"What aren't you telling me?" His eyes narrowed suspiciously.

The one thing I loved about Chad was that he never made me feel judged. He was laid back and chill, a nice balance to me. I often felt like I had my claws out, which worked out well for my job but horribly for relationships.

Every time I looked at him, I realized how good I had it. He was medium height, tanned from surfing, and nicely muscled from his job, and had sun-kissed light brown hair that was always a little too long. Most of the time, he had a goatee, but he'd shaved for this trip.

I sucked in a deep breath, deciding to go middle of the road in my response to his question. "I actually haven't told my parents that I'm married yet."

His mouth dropped open. "Are you serious?"

I nodded, guilt clawing at me. "Yes, I am. Unfortunately."

Sweat instantly formed on his brow. "So, we're going to show up at their front door and announce that I'm your husband?" He rubbed his chin. "This isn't going to go well. Why haven't you told them?"

"The truth?" I nibbled my lip, wishing I could magically transport myself from this conversation. For the past week, I'd felt nauseous at the thought of this trip. Only my parents could bring about this reaction in me.

"Of course."

"I'm terrified," I blurted.

"Terrified?" he repeated as if he hadn't heard correctly. "You're never scared."

"Except of my parents." He had no idea. I thought maybe it was better that way. He was happy go lucky, and I didn't want to get him worked up. Meeting the parents the first time was scary for anyone, but my parents made Godzilla seem kind and warm.

Chad reached over and squeezed my hand reassuringly. "I know you said they were kind of strict."

"They have unreasonably high expectations not only of how I should act, but of what I should do with my life."

"Right. So . . ." He twisted his lips. "I don't even know what to say."

"It's going to be fine." I wasn't convinced, but I didn't want him to know that. I hoped my tone didn't properly convey my true feelings.

"If you thought it would be fine, you would have told them already."

I couldn't even argue with that. I stared out the window at rural Connecticut in the fall. I should have felt invigorated by the picturesque surroundings, but instead I felt like I was about to enter a war zone that had been artfully disguised as a Norman Rockwell painting. "I wanted you to be by my side when I made the announcement."

"Because you're terrified?" he confirmed.

I nodded crisply. "Exactly."

He sighed. "This is going to be interesting. Where am I going, anyway?"

"Just a few more turns and we'll be there."

He glanced out the window as houses with spacious, well-manicured lawns began to dot the rolling landscape. "Nice neighborhood."

When I'd lived here, our ten-thousand-square-foot house, once owned by a four-star general, had been the only one on the street. In recent years, others had bought plots of land and built there. All the houses were large, but some more so than others.

"Turn here." I pointed to a street. It was my street, the place where I'd grown up. I was having trouble breathing as we started down the road. My heart beat erratically. Why did Chad have to insist on this trip? Why did he think it would be honorable to meet my folks? I would have been perfectly content to not see my parents again . . . for the rest of my life, basically.

But my sister Reina had called. It was my parents' fortieth wedding anniversary, and Reina insisted my brother and I be there to celebrate and honor my parents. Other distant relatives were also coming in, and a whole weekend of family time had been planned, including my parents renewing their vows.

I was only coming because I loved my sister. Reina was older by ten years and had practically been a second mother to me. She was quiet and didn't love managing people, so she'd decided against being a doctor. I suppose animals had seemed like an easier option, and vet school was close enough to med school that my parents were pleased. My mom was a pediatrician and my dad an oncologist.

Reina and I shared the love of animals, but otherwise we were opposites. Reina was reserved, compliant, and sweet. I was . . . none of those things.

Then there was my brother. He was single, eight years older than me, and a plastic surgeon living in New York City. I hadn't seen him in years, but he'd always had a way of making people feel like a million bucks, including me. However, during my formative years, he'd been sent off to boarding school, so in reality I felt closer to many of my friends than I did my own brother.

And that was my childhood in a nutshell.

Chad pressed on the brakes as the road ended at a glistening, paved driveway that looked fit for royalty. He stared up at the house at the end of the red-brick lane. "*This* is where you grew up? I thought you said it was small."

I looked at the massive structure and frowned. "It is small compared to a couple of the other houses on the street."

"I feel like I should have worn something other than my nicest surfing T-shirt." He tugged at the baby-blue jersey material. It was practically his uniform. Most of the time, neither of us had any need to dress up. We were casual and content to be that way.

I shook my head, shoving down any doubts about how presentable we were. "My family is going to have to accept you just as you are, and that's all there is to it."

I was independent and capable of making my own choices. My family was just going to have to adjust.

They were going to have to get used to Chad, for that matter.

Chad leaned closer and planted a quick kiss on my lips. "The fact that you love me just the way I am is just one more thing to love about you."

"I'm not in the business of changing people." I questioned the truth in my words. I actually tried to change people's minds all the time. I lived and breathed changing people's minds, for that matter.

"What was that?" Chad questioned.

"Okay, not changing *people*, per se. I just want to change the horrible practices concerning animals." That sounded a little better and didn't make me feel like such a dogmatic loon.

Chad nodded. "I get it, and I love you for it."

Chad put the van in park. The Vanagon looked out of place among a shiny BMW, a brand-new Volvo, and a luxury-class Lexus. Each of those vehicles was shiny, clean, and free of bumper stickers, colorful seat covers, and Hawaiian bobble-head dolls that danced with little persuasion.

We climbed out, and the midday sun hit our shoulders. It was brisk outside, but the cooler weather felt invigorating. I gulped some deep breaths of air. *I can do this!*

I took Chad's hand as we walked to the front door. It had been a long time since I'd been back here, and that was on purpose. I didn't have tons of great memories of my childhood. In fact, I'd run far from my family as soon as I'd been able to. There'd just been too much pressure, too much expectation, and too much absence to ever build bridges. I'd rejected nearly every part of my upbringing.

That's why I had no idea why I was standing here now, wearing my nicest jeans, a soft gray sweater, and my favorite pair of Converse All Stars. I tucked a black hair behind my ear and braced myself.

As the moment of reckoning came upon me, not even the lovely autumn weather could bring me any hope.

Before I even rang the bell, the intricate mahogany door opened and my longtime housekeeper from childhood stood there with a bright green feather duster in hand. "If it isn't my girl Sierra!"

The plump sixty-something woman pulled me into her arms and held me so tightly I felt like an anaconda had wrapped itself around my chest and squeezed. "Good to see you, Ms. Blankenship."

I coughed until finally my childhood equivalent of Mary Poppins let go. I resisted the urge to suck in deep, dramatic breaths, even though I kind of wanted to—make that *needed* to. All the air had been hugged out of my lungs.

She looked beyond me, her kind, grandmother-like eyes absorbing Chad. "And you must be her boyfriend."

Chad opened his mouth as if to correct her and then cast me a glance that spoke volumes. He did not like this, he didn't approve, and he probably didn't appreciate it. But he still stuck with me.

"Nice to meet you," he murmured instead, flashing a self-assured smile.

"Come on inside." She waved her feather duster and stepped back. "Everyone is waiting for you."

She ushered us in. As soon as I stepped foot into the tiled foyer of my parents' house, I felt like a child in elementary school who'd just done something wrong. I waited to be scolded, even though I had no idea why I might deserve it.

That's just the way it worked in my family. Whatever I did, I got in trouble for it. Looks of disapproval were commonly cast my way. I could handle scrutiny from almost anyone else, but receiving it from my family always put me over the edge.

I spotted several people milling around, mostly in the living room and kitchen, both of which I could see from the front door thanks to the open, airy design of the house. Everything in the house was clean and white or beige. Tall marble columns, shiny alabaster tile floors, whitewashed-framed pictures, ivory rugs, and creamy tables.

I'd always thought my mom decorated in this color scheme to make it easier to spot even a speck of dirt and freak out about it. She thought the house should be as clean as the operating room.

My mom and dad, who were sipping wine by the couch, spotted us first. My mom was a petite first-generation Japanese woman who loved business suits and practical high heels. Her hair was black and bobbed at her jawline, just as she'd always worn it. She also had reading glasses that she always wore on a chain around her neck. Since I'd seen her last, gray strands had streaked evenly through the black.

My mom had aged, I realized. Logically, I'd known that she would. But seeing her now caused an unknown emotion to crush against my heart.

Dad was also first-generation Japanese. He was short with graying hair and a pudge just starting at his stomach. He loved golf and jigsaw puzzles and rarely smiled. Maybe that made him good at his job as an oncologist.

The two had been childhood sweethearts and had moved to the States for medical school and ended up staying. They had their perfect family — my brother and sister. Then I came along accidentally eight years later. They had no idea what to do with me. I didn't fit into the busy schedule that was necessary for them both to be successful doctors. I'd been relegated to nannies and housekeepers and, eventually, sent off to boarding school.

Instead of throwing their arms around me — they weren't the type — they ambled over and looked Chad over like they were appraising a cow, trying to deem whether it was worthy of being sacrificed to their hunger.

When they finished, my mom raised her nose and

addressed me. "Sierra. So glad you could make it."

"Mom." I nodded properly, suddenly remembering my boarding school days, which I'd thought were long forgotten.

"Glad you could make it home, Sierra." My dad stood stiffly with one hand stuffed in his pocket.

"Of course. I wouldn't have missed it." I grabbed Chad's hand again, realizing that some time during this crazy exchange, I'd released it, perhaps as a subconscious way of buying time before I had to explain who the man beside me was. A sickly feeling gurgled in my stomach as I sucked in a deep breath. "Mother. Father. This is Chad."

I just couldn't bring myself to admit that we were married. Not yet. I wasn't ready for the fireworks that might explode. I needed to ease into this. Dip my toe into the water first.

Being timid was *so* not my thing. But my parents brought out a different side of me.

"Chad," my mom repeated with a curt nod. There was no "Nice to meet you" or "Pleasure to have you here." Instead, she stared, something in her gaze akin to a lion eyeing its prey.

"An old friend has stopped by to see you, Sierra," Dad announced. He cast a wary glance at Chad before looking back toward the kitchen.

I followed my father's gaze and sucked in a deep breath at the figure I saw standing there. "Greg?"

I hadn't seen him in . . . years. *Years*. Yet he still

looked the same. Five foot eight, thin with a head full of black hair and perceptive brown eyes. He wore a sweater vest, khakis, and sensible brown loafers.

Dread pooled in my stomach when I saw his face light with pleasure. I already regretted coming here. It was all a mistake. A big, horrible mistake.

Was it too late to turn around and run? We could just hop back in the Vanagon and drive all the way back to Virginia. That wouldn't be weird, right? I could pretend like this never happened and zoom back to my comfortable life, the life I'd made for myself away from my parents. A life that included being who I wanted to be, whether or not that involved making gobs of money or hanging out with connected, affluent people. I could be my own person with no one who mattered to judge me.

"Greg?" Chad whispered in my ear.

About that time, Greg strode across the room and stood in front of us. "Sierra Nakamura, you look just as lovely as ever." He took my hand and kissed it, his lips lingering a little too long.

I felt Chad bristle beside me, and I snatched my hand back.

"Greg, this is Chad. Chad, Greg." I didn't add that Greg was the man my parents had wanted me to marry. He was everything they thought was worthy in a good spouse: he was Asian, rich, and successful.

He was everything Chad wasn't. At least, in my parents' eyes.

Chad was a surfer, skier, former mortician, and present-day crime scene cleaner. We had very little in terms of material possessions, but we had everything in love. That's what really counted.

My parents would never, ever understand that, though.

"Greg has just joined Connecticut Pediatric Specialist Group," my mom continued. "He moved back to the area a few months ago. We knew as soon as we heard you were coming that the two of you would want to catch up."

Awkwardness fluttered both around me and inside me until I felt off balanced.

Everyone stared at me, maybe not realizing that I was way better at dealing with animals than I was people.

I had no idea what to say or do. I envied groundhogs. At the moment, I wanted to dig a hole and disappear.

"If it isn't Sierra!" a screechy voice said.

I didn't have to look to know that sound came from my crazy aunt Yori. She was my mom's older sister and lived in one of the spare bedrooms at the house. She'd been married once, but her husband died more than twenty years ago, and she had no kids. From as far back as I could remember, she'd been a little loopy.

She was the polar opposite of my mom. She was heavyset, had flyaway gray hair, and said whatever came to her mind—and she said it with flourish. For her entire life, she'd bounced from job to job, unable to maintain a steady career.

Right now, she charged toward me, her arms outstretched. She pulled me into a hug, pulled Chad into a hug, and then pulled me into a hug again. "You look good. Really good. Being away from home has treated you well, I see. Have you put on some weight?"

Tension pulled tight again. What did I say in response to her home comment? And had I put on weight? I didn't think I had, yet suddenly I felt fatter.

Thankfully, a squeal at the back door drew everyone's attention from me. I turned and saw a huge dog galloping inside. The brown-and-white canine had a mischievous glint to his eyes, a bounce in his gait, and a long tongue that hung out the side of his mouth.

My sister ran in behind him, her gaze frantic. "Stop him!"

The dog dodged several guests, sent one woman screaming and jumping on the couch like she'd seen a mouse, and nearly toppled Greg before coming to a stop directly in front of me. The canine sat down, tongue hanging out, and looked up at me as if I'd been his end goal this whole time.

My sister, usually composed and reserved, came to an abrupt stop behind him. She bent over, out of breath, and scowled at the dog before looking up at me. "Sierra, you're home. Welcome."

I fought a smile before rubbing the dog's head. He responded by leaning into me and eating up the attention. "Who's this?"

She shook her head, still gulping in air. "I have no idea. I found him in the backyard and tried to check his collar for tags. He wouldn't have anything to do with me. Then, as soon as I opened the door to come back inside and get help, he pushed by me, and now here he is."

I rubbed behind his ears some more. The dog's brown eyes were charming and intelligent. His coat had a smattering of brown dots in between swaths of chestnut and ivory. Floppy ears made him appear friendly and huggable.

"What a pretty boy," I murmured, more to the dog than anyone else.

When I looked over and saw my dad shielding my mom from the dog, I realized I needed to at least act more concerned. I reached down and checked the collar. There was no tag. It looked like there had been at one time, based on the silver half circle of wire with a gap in it. Maybe it had gotten hung up on something and ripped off.

"You ever seen him before?" I asked my parents.

"It's 'Have you ever seen him before?'" my mom corrected, stepping out from behind my father. "Certainly you haven't forgotten how to speak properly while living in Virginia?"

My cheeks heated, but I decided to ignore her. Respect was really important to my parents, so that meant not talking back and not embarrassing them in front of others. To do either of those things would be an atrocity to our already strained relationship.

"So, about the dog?" I questioned instead. "Have you ever seen him before?"

My mom shook her head, her lips pursed. "No, I have not."

"He couldn't have gone too far," Reina said, taking a better look. "His fur is still clean, not matted, and no burs are in it. I'd guess his home is close."

"What I don't understand is why that mutt is still inside my home!" my mom said, anger simmering in her voice.

"That's too bad. Things just got interesting, too," Aunt Yori muttered before hobbling back toward the kitchen.

I glanced at Chad, already feeling like I was suffocating here. I knew an escape route when I saw one. "You know what? The dog seems to like us. We'll see if we can find out where he lives."

"But you just arrived." My mom raised her hand, palm up, not in confusion but in exasperation.

I had to make sure this didn't look like I was desperate to get away—which I was—and instead appear like I was trying to be helpful. I'd had years to perfect this with my parents. "I know. But I can sense the stress the dog is causing here. We certainly can't put him out on the street. That would just be cruel. It should only take a few minutes to see if he lives nearby, and we'll be right back."

"Have it your way." My mom scowled and crossed her arms.

"We'll be back soon," I assured her. "I promise."

I grabbed the dog's thick collar and led him outside. As soon as the door closed behind me, I let out the breath I held and turned to Chad. "I am so sorry."

"I know you tried to warn me about your family, but wow. I thought you were exaggerating." His eyes were wide and maybe a little scared. Anyone in their right mind would feel the same way after the experience.

I shook my head, heading toward the van with the dog beside me. "I wish. It's not too late to turn around and run. What do you say?"

Hope invaded my voice. Maybe I didn't have to endure this weekend. Maybe we could say something came up back home, and we could hit the road again. My mind raced with ideas.

"What kind of impression would that leave? They'd really think I was good for nothing, a bad influence, and unfit for their daughter. And when exactly do you plan to tell them we're married again? That was never clear to me."

The knot in my stomach twisted tighter. I paused and laid a hand on his chest. "I will. I promise. I just have to wait for the right time."

"I hope the right time is before that Greg guy puts his lips against your hand again."

I shuddered, still moving toward the van. "That was

unfortunate."

"It's going to be unfortunate for him." He made a mockingly tough, angry face.

I knew Chad wasn't that kind of guy. But still, the whole encounter had been awkward.

"Chad —" I started to explain.

He opened the van. "I think I have a leash in here for the Bark in the Park event we went to."

Some of the tension left me. He wasn't bent out of shape — thank goodness. He was just joking. I couldn't handle another stressor at the moment.

"Found it." He emerged from the van's recesses with a bright blue lead with bones stamped down the side.

"You never know when one will come in handy. Isn't that what I always say?"

"Always." Humor dripped in his voice as he grabbed the leash and hooked it around the dog's neck. The canine sat down, looking up at us happily and panting.

"I wonder what kind he is. I'm thinking he's an English Spaniel. What do you think?" I patted him behind the ears again, and he raised his head as if to ask for more love and attention.

Chad leaned down to examine him more closely. "It's a good guess. Maybe a Welsh Springer Spaniel? Either way, pretty dog. He might be a purebred. A lady I used to work with at the funeral home had one of these. I think this breed is expensive."

"Breeds are just a ridiculous way of—"

He raised a hand, probably sensing I was about to launch into one of my speeches about the evils of dog breeding. "I know. Believe me, I know."

I straightened, trying to focus on the task ahead. "Before we go back to the pit of vipers known as my family, let's see if we can get Big Boy back home."

We started walking down the road, and I tried to ignore the sense of trepidation that filled me. I should have stuck to my guns, told Chad this was a horrible idea, and stayed in Virginia. But, no. I had to trek back up to my old home in Connecticut and reconnect with my family.

Growing up, Mom and Dad had worked too much. I'd been raised by a series of nannies and comforted from my nightmares not by people but by my cats— usually strays that I snuck inside and nurtured back to health.

My parents had wanted me to follow in their footsteps and go into the medical field. Instead, I'd horrified them by becoming an animal rights activist. Even my recent promotion to director of the organization probably wouldn't impress them.

"Why don't we start here?" Chad said, pausing by a Georgian-style house with highly impressive flower beds. A cheerful green Volkswagen Beetle was parked in the driveway with a "Here Comes Treble" bumper sticker.

We crossed the manicured lawn, Big Boy walking

happily beside us. I noticed he didn't particularly pull us toward the door, as if he was familiar with it, or like a horse running home. Animals had those kinds of instincts. He seemed content by our side instead.

We tried the house anyway, despite my gut feeling that this wasn't the place. We rang the doorbell, and before we could even step back, a woman answered. She had a bundle of red curly hair atop her head and wore a sleek pantsuit. "Can I help you?"

"We found this dog and we're looking for his owner," I started. "We're going door to door to see if anyone recognizes him."

Her gaze fluttered down toward the dog. "I do believe he belongs to the Lennoxes. They're two doors down in the house with the blue shutters and slightly overgrown grass."

"Thank you," I called as we started down the steps.

"You must be one of the Nakamuras," she called behind me, her voice sounding uninterested, a stark contrast to the fact that she was trying to continue the conversation.

I paused. "I'm their daughter."

"Well, God bless you, then." She turned her nose up and shut the door.

Apparently, my family had made quite the impression on this street. Wasn't that just fantastic?

We continued through the neighborhood until we reached the house with the blue shutters and the slightly overgrown grass. The first thing I noticed was that the front door was cracked open. Second, I noticed the trail of blood leading down the front walk, stopping at the very place on the driveway where a car had probably been parked.

Before I could voice my observations, Big Boy let out a long-drawn-out howl.

Realization dawned in my gut, spreading through me until mourning captured every cell.

Big Boy knew something we didn't.

He knew that something was seriously wrong.

CHAPTER 2

"We should call the police," I muttered, my gaze fixated on the trail of blood.

"You call the police. I'm going to check inside and make sure no one is hurt," Chad said. "We don't know for sure if that blood is leading to or from the house."

With trembling hands, I pulled my phone out and dialed 911. After taking a breath to calm myself, I explained to the operator what had happened, and she promised that the police were on the way.

I stood on the lawn for a moment with a howling Big Boy. Each second I heard the sound only compounded my emotions. I found myself inching closer to the house.

What was taking Chad so long? Was he okay? What if a killer was still inside?

The thought caused my heart to lurch into my throat.

Though something in my subconscious urged me to stop before I did something stupid, I crept toward the front door. Big Boy stayed at my side.

I reached the porch and, with hesitant movements, peeked inside the lavish house. "Chad?"

No answer.

As more trepidation filled me, I took another step. My gaze perused the entryway. It was a contrast to my parents' house. The walls were painted pumpkin orange and other jewel tones. Everything was accented with dried flowers and artfully arranged vases of sticks.

There, in front of me, was that trail of blood. Not a stream. Not a line. Just small drops sprinkled like bread crumbs.

Something bad had happened here.

Almost in a trancelike state, I began following the path across the bamboo floor. I walked through the entryway and toward the living room on the far side of the house. I made sure that Big Boy stayed far away from the blood so we disturbed nothing.

A deep voice startled me. "What are you doing?"

I twirled around and saw Chad standing at the base of the stairs. My hand covered my heart, which now beat double time. "You scared me to death."

"I thought you were waiting outside," he said.

"I got worried when I didn't hear anything."

He closed the distance between us. "The house is empty. There's no one here."

"Any signs of foul play?" I asked.

He shook his head. "No. Just that blood. It starts in the kitchen and ends at the driveway. Otherwise, I haven't seen anything out of the ordinary."

"Strange. Big Boy definitely thinks something is wrong." I absently rubbed the dog's head again.

Chad took my elbow. "Let's wait outside for the police to come. The last thing we need is for them to tell us we compromised a crime scene."

***

Fifteen minutes later the police arrived. We explained to the detective in charge what had happened, and she took our statements. She'd introduced herself as Detective Meadows. She was on the tall side, extremely thin, and probably in her early thirties. She had long blonde hair that had been pulled into a bun, and didn't wear any makeup. Her oversized suit made her look a bit dowdy, but she seemed to know what she was doing.

Thank goodness Big Boy had stopped howling, because the sound chilled me to the bone. Dogs had that instinct to know when bad things happened. If only Big Boy could talk now, maybe there wouldn't be so many questions.

As the police worked the scene, I stood back on the sidewalk watching everything. That's when I spotted a familiar figure walking down the lane.

My sister.

Her eyes widened when she saw the police cars. By the time she reached us, she looked overly concerned. "I heard the commotion at the end of the street. Mom and Dad sent me to make sure everything was okay."

Of course, Mom and Dad didn't come themselves,

so they weren't *that* worried. I cast aside those thoughts. I couldn't live in bitterness and resentment. And, what I already had of those emotions, I had to channel into protecting the rights of neglected and abused animals.

That was the key. Using the negative in your life for good. For me, that translated into taking forgotten animals and loving on them. Stopping circuses from treating animals like objects. Preventing pet stores from seeing furry creatures as a means to make profit — whatever the cost.

"Apparently, this is where Big Boy lives," I told Reina. "The door was open when we got here, and we found blood."

"You're traumatized, aren't you?" She leaned down and rubbed the dog's head. "He really likes you, Sierra. You've always been an animal magnet."

"Poor thing is sad right now." I frowned at the dog, wishing I could speak to him and that my words would make sense enough to ease his troubled heart. "He knows."

Just then, an oversized SUV that could have been part of the presidential motorcade screeched in front of the house. A man in his forties stormed toward the crowd on the lawn. He had thinning brown hair, narrow shoulders, and a slightly hooked nose. His button-up shirt and loose-fitting tie seemed to indicate he'd been working.

"What is going on here?" he demanded. His voice

sounded too high and soft for him to be scary. But he did appear to be wound up like a snake about to strike.

The detective stepped out of the crowd. "Sir, who are you?"

"I live here! I'm Reggie Lennox. Someone tell me what's going on."

"Mr. Lennox, we found blood leading down your driveway, and a concerned neighbor called the police."

"A concerned neighbor? None of my neighbors have ever cared anything about me, except if I let my grass grow too long!" Veins bulged at his temples, and his eyes looked wide enough to pop out.

Big Boy remained by my side. I made a mental note that he wasn't running toward his owner as most dogs would.

"Do you have any idea how the blood got here?" Detective Meadows continued, pointing toward the red drops on the ground.

"That?" His voice rose like an angry hyena, and he pointed to his face. "I got a nosebleed. I decided to go to the store and get some more vitamin C. It seems to work for me whenever I have this problem."

I remembered the dots of blood. Perhaps they were small enough for a nosebleed. Had all of this been a huge misunderstanding? One that I instigated, at that?

"I'm sorry that you had to waste the police department's valuable resources and time, but you can all leave now," Mr. Lennox continued. "I've got to get back to work."

"We just have a few more questions. Does anyone live here with you, Mr. Lennox?" Detective Meadows continued.

He stopped and sighed, making it clear that we were a big nuisance to him. "Yes, my wife. But she's out of town on business."

"When will she return?"

"Not until next week."

"What's the nature of her business?"

"She's at a trade show this week in Atlanta. She works in public relations." He glanced at his watch. "Any more questions, because I've got a phone conference in five minutes, and I can't be late."

"We're sorry to have disturbed you," the detective said. "Please, carry on."

The man stormed inside and slammed his front door. Just as Detective Meadows began walking toward the police sedan, I stepped forward. "Detective?"

She paused and turned to look at me. "Yes?"

"Aren't you going to collect any evidence?"

She shook her head. "There hasn't been a crime here."

"How can you be so sure?"

"A little blood isn't indicative that something bad happened, Mrs. Davis."

Crud! The officer had used my married name. I glanced back at my sister, hoping she hadn't heard it.

Of course she had. She stared at me now, her eyes wide. She was no dummy, so I had no doubt she'd put things together. I'd worry about that in a minute.

"You're just going to take his word for it?" I continued.

The detective shifted, obviously annoyed. "What do you suggest?"

"I'd make sure that blood is really his."

"There's no probable cause."

"Sure there is." I pointed to Big Boy. "He howled."

"And that proves . . . ?"

"Dogs can sense death." I thought everyone knew that.

She stared at me like I'd lost my mind. "I think you're reading too much into this."

"I don't think you're reading enough into this," I argued back.

Chad took my arm and pulled me back.

"Thanks for coming out," he said to Detective Meadows, a calm, professional tone to his voice. "We appreciate all you've done."

Before I could say anything else, he nudged me away.

"What are you doing?" I asked him, desperately wanting to finish my conversation with the detective.

"I'm trying to keep you from being arrested," he whispered.

"Arrested? Why would she arrest me? She needs to arrest that man."

"The detective is right. There's no evidence that something is wrong. People hurt themselves all the time. Just because there's blood on the ground doesn't mean a crime occurred. And if you keep being pushy with the detective, she's going to have you in her sights."

Begrudgingly, I nodded. "Fine."

But in my head, nothing was fine.

CHAPTER 3

As the police pulled away, I looked down at Big Boy and frowned. "I guess his people companion wasn't in a hurry to get this lovable furball inside. Mr. Lennox didn't even ask what we were doing with him."

Chad reached for him. "I'll take him to Mr. Lennox."

"He's on a conference call." My grip instinctively tightened on the leash.

"He's not our dog, Sierra," Chad reminded me sternly.

"But the man obviously doesn't care about him." My voice rose with conviction. "When you care about something or someone, you just don't leave them panting outside with strangers."

"Chad, make a mental note to never leave Sierra in the yard without any water," my sister said with a touch of amusement in her voice.

I dropped my head toward my shoulder, hoping to look no-nonsense. "You know what I mean."

"If we take the dog back to your parents, it would be like stealing—or dognapping, for that matter," Chad reminded me, saying each word slowly. "We can't do that."

"Besides, Mom and Dad hate dogs. You know that," Reina reminded me.

Part of me wanted to cross my arms and pout. But I knew that wouldn't get me anywhere. The idea of animals being mistreated brought out all different sides of my personality—from the aggressive side to the juvenile. Really, on average, I was an even-keeled person who'd graduated at the top of my class from Yale.

"Okay," I finally said. Reluctantly, I handed over Big Boy to Chad. Before Chad pulled him away, I leaned down until I was nose to wet nose with the dog. "You take care of yourself, okay?"

Big Boy whined and licked my cheek. Chad tugged at the leash. I frowned before releasing the dog. I had to look away as Chad climbed the porch steps.

My sister leaned closer. "Did that detective call you Mrs. Davis?"

I shrugged, my attention turning to my other problems for a moment. "Maybe."

"Why would she do that?" She raised an eyebrow.

"I may have . . ." I wanted to take the easy road and mumble a response she wouldn't understand. Instead, I blurted, ". . . gotten married."

I pressed my lips together as I waited for her response.

"You didn't tell Mom and Dad?" my sister hissed, her eyes wide.

"I haven't yet, and you can't tell them either. I'm waiting for just the right moment."

"That's usually before you say 'I do.' *That's* the right moment."

I narrowed my eyes. "I know. I know. But—" I glanced back at Chad and lowered my voice. "You know Mom and Dad."

She nodded adamantly. "Yes, I sure do. And when you finally tell them, it's not going to be good. And what about Greg? You don't think he's here by accident, do you? This is not good!"

She didn't have to tell me that. I already knew. "I'll handle it. Just promise me you'll stay quiet."

"You know I can't lie." She crossed her arms.

My sister was Mrs. Prim-and-Proper, straight and narrow, black and white.

"I'm not asking you to lie. I'm just asking you to avoid this subject. It's not like Mom and Dad will ask out of the blue if Chad and I are married."

Reina scowled but finally nodded. "I'll do my best to stay quiet. I don't like this, though."

Our attention was drawn to the front door. Reggie Lennox didn't look too happy with Chad. "I'm on a conference call. Do you understand what that is, surfer boy?"

"Look, I thought you might want your dog back." Chad's shoulders tensed.

Reggie narrowed his eyes at the dog. "How'd you get your hands on him, anyway?"

"He was roaming the street."

"Oh." Mr. Lennox snatched the leash. "I suppose this is where I should say thank you."

He pulled the dog inside and slammed the door.

More than anything, I wanted to run up to the door and take Big Boy back. But that wasn't a possibility. Well, it was, but I'd be arrested. That really would make an impression on my parents, wouldn't it?

"That man has anger management issues," Chad muttered as he cut across the lawn to meet us.

I kept my eye on the door. "I agree."

Just then, Big Boy appeared in the window. He barked as he watched us walk down the street.

"I feel awful leaving him," I said, unable to pull my gaze away.

Chad squeezed my hand but said nothing.

"Rehearsal dinner starts in an hour and a half," Reina reminded us. "Why don't you think about the dog after that?"

"I just don't buy that man's story," I mumbled, barely hearing my sister.

"But what can you do?" Chad asked. "You have to leave it to the police. You have to trust that they know how to do their jobs."

"I suppose."

But I often found that if I wanted something done right, I had to do it myself.

***

An hour later, I stepped from my bedroom, freshly showered and focused again on honoring my parents this weekend. My stomach still seemed a bit queasy despite willing myself to relax.

After Chad and I had returned, we unloaded the suitcases from the van. Mother had ordered Chad to follow her after instructing me that I'd been assigned to my childhood bedroom. I made a quick stop in the kitchen to drop off some vegan food items like soy cheese and black bean burgers that I'd brought along, just to make sure I had something to eat while here.

After showering, I waited to meet Chad in the upstairs hallway. The place had always reminded me of a museum corridor with all its fancy pictures with gold frames, freshly waxed trim, and intricately designed carpet. I straightened my wine-colored dress for rehearsal dinner, wondering if I had put an extra pound or two onto my petite frame. Maybe Aunt Yori was right.

I saw Chad approaching on the other side of the hallway, only he didn't come from the direction of one of the bedrooms on that side of the house, near Ms. Blankenship's quarters. He approached me from the bottom of the staircase, looking none too happy.

"Different rooms I would have understood. But the guesthouse? Really, Sierra?" Chad whispered as we met in the hallway.

I straightened Chad's ocean-blue tie. "It's a delicate

situation." I didn't add that I was certain the placement was a calculated move on my mom's part.

"I guess so, because I've never seen you so insecure. You're Mrs. I Know What I Want. Being around your family makes you jumpier than a bunch of monkeys at a slumber party."

"When you're around people who don't believe in you and whom you've severely disappointed with your life choices, it's easy to get that way." It was meant to sound light. Instead, I feared I sounded pathetic and a little too exposed.

He rubbed my arms. "Well, I miss my old Sierra. The one who's not afraid of anything, but who has a heart of gold. She's smart, beautiful, and concerned about the world around her."

"That's me." My voice lacked conviction at the moment.

He shook his head. "I don't know. I think that Sierra took a vacation somewhere else. Hawaii, maybe. But she's not here in Connecticut."

"I'd much rather be in Hawaii."

"Meanwhile, I'm sleeping in the other wing while my wife sleeps amongst her old dolls and stuffed animals."

I placed my hand on his chest. "We'll survive for the weekend. You look handsome, by the way."

"You always look beautiful." He leaned down to kiss me when I heard a footfall down the hall.

We both straightened when we spotted my tiger

mom walking our way. Her gaze flickered from Chad to me, and I instantly stepped away from my husband.

"You look nice, Mother." My voice took on a much more proper tone than usual.

And she did. She wore a silk pale pink number that accentuated her slim figure. She nodded stiffly. "Sierra. Chad. You both clean up nicely. Are you ready to run through the ceremony downstairs?"

I nodded. "Of course. Can't wait."

"*I* can't wait. Please use complete sentences, Sierra. I feel the need to repeat myself. Virginia has been a bad influence on you. Do people not speak properly down there?"

"Yes, they speak properly, Mother. With people I know well, I usually let down my guard and speak more casually." Mistake!

"We raised you better than that. Always put your best foot forward. Always." Her bristly gaze latched onto mine.

I held my chin up higher and stole a glance at Chad. His eyes were wide in astonishment. My mom could shake up even the most laid-back person.

We followed her downstairs, Chad attempting to make polite—and proper—conversation about how nice her house was, how beautiful the autumn leaves were, and how grateful he was to be a part of this weekend. Finally, we reached the backyard.

Rows of white chairs had been set up there in anticipation of tomorrow's event. A priest stood in the stage area, which was framed with a white pergola. White tulle was tucked between various eaves and nooks. Whether I wanted to admit it or not, the ceremony was going to be lovely. Even if my parents had chosen to release monarch butterflies at the end of it. I knew for a fact that hundreds of the insects, which had been delivered earlier, were sitting on ice packs in the garage at the moment, in a state of frozen limbo. Talk about cruel and inhumane.

But I needed to honor my parents. I had to keep reminding myself of that. This weekend was about them, not me.

As I paused at the edge of the deck, a woman with a pale blue suit who wore her brown hair in a French twist and carried a clipboard under her arm approached me. The wedding planner. It seemed like I'd heard her name earlier as I'd been ushered inside the house with my luggage, but I couldn't remember it for the life of me.

Charo or something crazy? She looked like a Charo with her big hair, tight "business" suit, painfully high heels, and overdone makeup.

"I'm Sierra," I told her.

She held out a limp hand. "Pleasure. I'm Charo."

"Charo?" I clarified.

"No, Sharo, with an *S.*"

I felt like I'd just shaken hands with a jellyfish. Where did my mom and dad find this lady?

She tugged on my dress at the waistline. "You

know, with a little altering, this would be a lot more flattering."

I looked down at my knee-length gown. "I think it fits pretty well."

"Trust me, you should show off your curves more. Especially if you want to get the guys." She raised her eyebrows suggestively.

"I'll keep that in mind." I wouldn't be having my dress altered, despite what she said.

"I used to be in fashion, so I know a thing or two about the way clothing should fit."

"Good to know."

"Isn't it?" She grinned and glanced at her watch. "Okay, it looks like it's showtime." As quickly as she'd begun the conversation, she turned and clapped her hands. "All right, everyone in place!"

I took my spot next to my sister on the stage area while Chad sat in the audience.

While Sharo shouted instructions, I glanced around. Even in the autumn, the grass looked thick and green. Woods stood like a guard at the back of the property, the trees glorious shades of red, orange, and yellow. White pickets lined the perimeter, while privacy fences bordered the yard next to the neighbors'.

A small guesthouse was to the left, beside a soaking pool, complete with a waterfall cascading into it. In the side yard, my parents had Japanese maple trees, a small bridge, and a reflection pond, all beautifully maintained.

"How are we being seated?" Aunt Yori asked a little too loudly. She stood in the center of the aisle, squinting against the sun at everyone onstage.

Sharo paused, looking flustered for a moment. "What do you mean?"

"I mean, will extended family wait to be seated at the beginning of the ceremony? It's not rocket science."

I cringed at her tone.

"It's whatever the Nakamuras prefer," Sharo said. She turned to my parents. "Preference?"

"Whatever is normal," my mother said.

She glanced at her clipboard and swallowed hard. "Okay then, immediate family will be seated first, followed by extended family. Sound good?"

I was no expert, but that order didn't seem normal. The answer seemed like it should be basic knowledge for someone who did this for a living.

As Sharo continued to talk, my gaze scanned the crowd. I spotted Reina's husband, Mark, as well as some aunts and uncles. Some of my parents' colleagues were there, including Dr. Moto, my official godfather, even though I'd only seen him on special occasions and felt absolutely no connection with him. My brother, on the other hand, still hadn't shown up.

Greg also sat there, on the opposite side of the aisle from Chad.

He waved when I looked his way.

I attempted a feeble smile and fluttered my hands in the air. Then I looked at Chad and saw him scowl.

Oh, what fun.

Just as we began to run through the ceremony, I noticed movement in the distance. I held my breath, trying to comprehend what was happening.

"Then you'll both say the vows you've written for each other," the priest said.

At once, it clicked in my head what was unfolding. Big Boy had returned. He leaped over the fence and galloped right toward my parents.

I raised my hand in horror. "No!"

It was too late. He dashed onstage, mud flying off him and splattering everywhere.

My mom screamed. My dad tried in vain to block him. Mark attempted a tackle maneuver.

But Big Boy didn't stop. Not until he reached me and had left a trail of dirt in his wake.

He sat down proudly and dropped something at my feet.

It was a bone.

I was just guessing, but I felt certain it wasn't any ordinary bone. Based on the size and shape, it was human.

CHAPTER 4

"What is that dog doing?" my always-serious mom screeched. My mom hardly ever screeched. Like, ever. She had the talent of calmly saying words and striking fear into people.

"I'll handle him," I insisted, casting a quick glance at Chad.

He took his cue and sprang from his seat to join me onstage. Holding the dog by the collar, I leaned toward Chad.

"Check out the bone," I whispered.

His eyes narrowed as he comprehended my words. He squatted and examined Big Boy's gift. When Chad stood, I could tell his evaluation matched mine. "We're going to have to call the police. That's human. A femur."

A couple of people gasped. Several screamed. Nearly everyone backed away—except Aunt Yori. She clapped and said, "Now things are getting interesting."

I stole another glance down and cringed. That bone didn't look all that old. In fact, there was still some pink stuff attached to it. Yuck.

I thought of Mr. Lennox, and then I thought about

his wife, who was supposed to be out of town. Why did I have a feeling that wasn't the case at all?

"How do you know that's human?" the priest asked.

"The size, the porousness," Chad said. "It's definitely human."

Reina stood by my parents with her cell phone to her ear, and I assumed she was calling the police.

"Please, get that dog out of here, Sierra." My mom pounced on each word before glancing at me like this was all my fault. I had nothing to do with this. Not this time.

I took a deep breath to compose myself. "How about if I take him to the garage? Would that be okay?"

"Fine," my dad said.

"Guard the bone, but don't touch it," I told my sister.

She nodded.

I led Big Boy across the lawn. Everyone we passed recoiled in horror as if the dog was some kind of serial killer. Poor Big Boy. He was just doing what canines did — digging and following scents.

I had a feeling this dog was trying to get a message across. I felt like he was silently pleading for my help somehow.

My dad appeared beside me with a key in hand. "I'll unlock it."

"Do you always lock the garage?"

"I lock up everything. We've had copper thefts in

the area recently. Once crime starts to grow, it continues. Before long, those leeches will try to get into our home to steal things as well."

"Copper thefts, huh? I've heard they're becoming a common problem." I wanted to keep talking, but I knew I was trying too hard. "It looks like a nice ceremony. The wedding planner is a trip. Where did you guys meet her?"

"Your mother ran into her while she was having her dress altered. She just happened to be in the shop, working for another client, and overheard your mother talking."

I stepped inside the tidy space, and before my dad could separate himself from the living, breathing—not to mention furry—disaster, I stopped him. "By the way, I met your neighbor today. Mr. Lennox."

My dad raised his chin, his eyebrow twitching like it always did when he didn't approve. "Yes, I know him."

"What do you know about him?" I continued, shutting the door behind me before Big Boy could escape again. "He seemed peculiar."

"I don't know, Sierra." Exasperation saturated his voice as he flipped the lights on. "He's married. No kids. They keep to themselves. Unlike our other neighbor, Mrs. Jericho."

"I think I met her also. The redhead?" I remained in the entryway, still holding on to Big Boy so he wouldn't mess up the pristine space. Garages should not be this clean.

His eyebrow twitched again as he reached for the doorknob. "She's the most obnoxious woman I've ever had the displeasure of meeting. All she does is complain about everyone else in the neighborhood. She's single with nothing better to do, I suppose."

"I'm sorry to hear that." I had to turn the topic of conversation back to a potential murder, though, especially in light of that bone. Plus, my dad seemed anxious to get out of here. "But about the Lennoxes . . ."

"I don't know much about them, Sierra."

"Did they seem to get along?"

He tilted his head as if suddenly realizing where I was going with these questions. "Why are you talking in past tense? Do you think that bone belongs to one of them?"

"Mr. Lennox said his wife was out of town. Plus, I saw blood at their home. He claims he had a bloody nose, but I don't know if I believe him, not in light of this new development."

He put his hand on my shoulder. "Sierra, leave the investigating to the police. You just worry about these vows we're renewing. Your mother wants everything to be perfect, and so far, that's not the case."

"I'm sorry, Dad."

He squeezed. "It's not your fault. But I just know this means a lot to her. I want her to feel special and for nothing to go wrong."

For nothing to go wrong. I nodded, my gut telling me

that was about as likely to happen as me finding a genie in a bottle and him granting me a wish for all the puppy mills to close forever.

***

The same detective from earlier showed up ten minutes later, along with some crime scene techs. One CSI took pictures and collected the bone, while two others had taken Big Boy outside and were pulling things off his fur. Apparently, the lighting in the garage was insufficient, and they were afraid they might miss something.

"Do you think it's a human bone?" Detective Meadows asked one of her colleagues.

The stocky officer beside her shrugged. "No idea."

"That's definitely a human bone," Chad said. "Unless Bigfoot is hiding out here in the woods of Connecticut, that is. No other animals native to this area would have bones that size."

"I concur," Greg said, puffing his chest out. "He's telling the truth. I'm a doctor, so I have experience with these types of things."

Everyone turned to Chad, and he shrugged. "I used to be a mortician, so I have my fair share of experience as well."

I waited for Chad to cast Greg a dirty look, but he didn't look at all fazed by the one-upmanship of my ex-boyfriend. Instead, I found myself scowling at both men.

"You know what the old man thinks?" Aunt Yori said.

We all waited. I, for one, had no idea who the old man was she was referring to, but maybe she had some great insight.

She raised her eyebrows. "He would say that the knee bone's connected with the thighbone. The thighbone's connected to the hip—" My aunt started doing a dance as her words moved into song.

"Yori!" my mother said, her mouth parting in horror.

Yori shrugged. "What?"

Detective Meadows cleared her throat and maybe— just maybe—rolled her eyes a little as she turned away from us. "We need to figure out where this dog got the bone."

"The old man gave it to him," Yori continued.

Everyone turned to her again, waiting to hear her revelation.

"What old man?" the detective asked.

"The one that does everything with a knickknack and paddy wack."

"Please, someone get her out of here," Detective Meadows mumbled.

My sister led her away. As I heard my aunt singing "Dem Bones" again, I couldn't help but smile. Things were always interesting when she was around.

The detective turned to the stocky sidekick officer

again. "Your wife has a poodle, right?"

The officer gave a halfhearted shrug. "Yeah."

"Great. Since you're a dog person, maybe you can get our four-legged friend to lead you to the location of origin."

"With the right motivation, the big pooch might do just that." The officer reached into his pocket, fumbled around, and then pulled something out. He dangled a candy bar toward Big Boy. "I've got something good for you to eat, little buddy."

Horror washed over me, and I slapped the candy out of his hand. It was time to end this comedy of errors. "Stop! Chocolate kills dogs. Don't you know that?"

He withdrew his hand. "It was the only thing I had in my pocket."

I shook my head. Anyone with common sense knew not to give dogs chocolate. "May I?"

"May you what?" Detective Meadows asked, eyeing me suspiciously.

I pointed toward the dog. "May I see if the dog will lead me to the crime scene? Big Boy seems to like me."

The detective and the officer exchanged a look before finally Detective Meadows nodded. "I suppose that will be fine, as long as you promise not to disturb anything at the scene. The dog does seem attached to you."

"I just need to change first."

The detective nodded. I grabbed Chad's hand and

whispered an update to him as I pulled him inside. He was coming with me, whether he wanted to or not.

We met downstairs five minutes later. I tromped past the neat white chairs, filled with everyone who'd waited in limbo to hear what was going on. My mom had taken a seat in the back row and looked both tired and agitated. I actually felt a little bad for her.

I knew this was supposed to be her rehearsal and the rehearsal dinner. But there could be a dead body out there, I reminded myself. I couldn't just ignore that. With any luck, I'd be back before anyone lifted a fork to partake of the dead pig that had been roasting in the backyard all day. With scents like that, it was no wonder Big Boy was drawn to this property.

When I reached the dog, who stood with the detective and officer by the guesthouse, I bent down to look him in the eye. "You ready to do this, boy?"

He wagged his tail and barked.

Chad had grabbed the leash from the van and put it on his collar. I took a hold of it, and as soon as I did, Big Boy started pulling me out of the backyard. Everyone behind me scrambled to keep up.

He led me through the back gate, into the woods, deeper into the woods, and over a small stream. He didn't let up but seemed to know exactly where he was going. I just held on for the ride.

Finally, he came to a stop beside an enormous stump and barked. I looked back at Detective Meadows. "I'd start here."

The detective and a couple of the crime scene techs rounded the remains of an old tree. As they did, a stench rose up, nearly making me gag. Dried leaves? Rotting trees? Decaying animals?

I knew that wasn't the case.

One of the crime scene techs pulled his nose back and closed his eyes.

"You were right," he said. "That dog led us right to the body."

CHAPTER 5

I couldn't get the body out of my mind. I hadn't actually seen it myself. No, the officers had led Chad and me away so we wouldn't compromise any evidence. Based on their description and the smell, it was better that way. I did overhear them say that Big Boy wasn't the only one who'd discovered it. Apparently, nature and all the critters in the forest had been very busy also.

The police had also insisted on keeping Big Boy with them so they could collect a stool sample. They'd said something about him potentially eating evidence. I'd argued that I could keep him, but the police hadn't backed down. Detective Meadows said the dog would be back home at the Lennoxes' by tomorrow if everything went well.

I felt like I was leaving behind a helpless child as I walked away. Everything felt a bit surreal, like a bad dream or a vivid movie. But the events of today had really happened.

Chad and I tromped through the woods hand in hand back toward my parents'. "You know what this reminds me of?" Chad asked.

"One of those real-life crime shows on TV?"

He shook his head. "No, it reminds me of when we were doing that video shoot for one of your mini documentaries on the Hessel's Hairstreak butterfly, and we found . . ."

He didn't have to finish. The moment flashed back to me, and I cringed. "Yeah, how could I forget that? I guess I have a knack for finding dead bodies."

"I thought Gabby was the only one good at that. Your discovery rate is starting to rival hers."

Gabby was my best friend, and she always knew what to do when she stumbled upon crimes. That trait served her well, since she wanted to go into forensics. She just had to find someone who would hire her now.

For a minute, I wished she was here so I could ask her advice. But she was attending to other matters at home: primarily taking care of her fiancé, who'd been shot in the head by a homicidal maniac.

I felt bad for my friend. She'd been through so much and never seemed to catch any breaks. If it weren't for Gabby, Chad and I would probably have never met. The two of them had been friends first, but when Chad and I ran into each other after a whale beached itself on the shores of the Chesapeake Bay, we'd instantly bonded. We'd been together ever since. Some people might even say we'd gotten married quickly, without even dating six months. But when someone knows they've found "the one," why put it off?

"You think that woman back there in the woods is Mrs. Lennox, don't you?" Chad asked.

"Makes sense to me, at least based on the evidence I've seen so far. An irate husband, a blood trail, an open door. Put it together and what do you have? A crime."

"It's certainly made this trip more interesting, not that the trip needed any help."

I barely heard him. "I say we go pay him a visit."

"Who?"

"Mr. Lennox." I nodded, convinced I was right.

"Visit Mr. Lennox and say what?" Something that sounded close to anxiety edged into his voice.

I shrugged as I climbed over a fallen tree, my thoughts already racing ahead in time. "Get our leash back . . . and tell him that we found his dog, who is now in police custody."

"You want to accuse him of murder? Tip him off that the cops may show up? Maybe we should let the police make the next play."

I sighed in thought. Chad had a point. "We can come in sympathy. Keep any judgment from our voices. Make it sound like we thought he knew."

"Or we could be impeding a police investigation," Chad reminded me.

He sounded so knowledgeable. "You're so sexy when you talk like that."

He perked. "Really? Because I can use police speak all you want. Copy that?"

I elbowed him. "I'm afraid that dog's going to get

the short end of the—"

"Bone?"

"Stick. Short end of the stick. I'd hate to see Big Boy end up in a shelter."

"Is that his name? Big Boy?"

I shook my head. "That's what I call him. I think it fits."

He groaned, holding aside a low-lying branch as I ducked under. "Oh no. You're already bonding with him. You know we can't have a dog in the apartment building. Besides, he'd try to eat your cats. I mean, *our* cats." He cleared his throat.

"What kind of person would I be if I didn't at least try to help, though?"

Chad raised his hand. "I'm not suggesting that we don't help. We just have to keep a cool head here."

"That's my middle name. Sierra Never-a-Hot-Head Davis."

He chuckled, and we quickly detoured from our path toward my parents'. We headed toward the Lennoxes' backyard instead. As we scuttled past my family's property, I heard the murmur of guests at the rehearsal dinner. It sounded like they'd continued their party. Maybe things weren't as jolly as they could have been, but maybe also my mom and dad would be less inclined to notice I was gone.

"See that tarp and wheelbarrow in the backyard?" I asked Chad as we got closer to Big Boy's home. The items in question were located behind the shed, tucked away out of sight.

"What about them?"

"I don't see where Mr. Lennox has been working on any landscaping recently. All his plants and trees look pretty well established." I surveyed the area to confirm that my initial impressions were correct. Everything — even the grass — looked fully grown. There was no fresh dirt anywhere or any other signs that someone had been gardening.

"Don't jump to conclusions. He didn't necessarily use that to dump his wife's dead body."

"I'm not doing any jumping. I'm just pointing out facts. There's a difference." I made sure we detoured past the equipment on our way to the front door. I paused behind the shed and got a better look.

Chad pointed to a dark brown stain on the blue tarp. "You're right. The police might want to check this out."

I cringed when I saw it. Dried blood? I couldn't be sure, but certainly the police had tests to determine what it was. The splotches were definitely too big for a nosebleed.

This man was getting creepier and creepier by the minute.

I hurried past the enormous deck and around the side of the house and charged up to the front door. I reminded myself to look compassionate and not like someone who was out for blood — which seemed to be the extent of my relationship with Mr. Lennox so far.

I rang the bell before Chad even caught up with me.

Mr. Lennox answered, still wearing the same outfit from earlier. He narrowed his eyes when he saw me. "You. What do you want this time? Did you bring the police again? Report I had a boo-boo on my knee and demand an investigation?"

Nice, Sierra. Be nice, even in the face of mean, spiteful people.

"I just saw your dog running through the woods behind my parents' house. I wanted to make sure he was okay."

He grunted, his beady eyes not showing an ounce of compassion. "I'm sure he's fine."

He started to shut the door.

"Wait!" I cried.

He paused and tapped his foot.

I had to think quickly. "I just don't want to see anything happen to Big Boy."

"Who's Big Boy?" He spit out the words, looking at me like I'd lost my mind.

"I mean . . . I mean, your dog, who just happens to *be* a big boy. Anyway, stray dogs often end up in shelters, if not worse. I'd hate for the dogcatcher to come."

He sighed and leaned against the door. "Do you have a point? I'm a very busy man with much better things to do than have this conversation."

I shook my head. "Only that dogs shouldn't roam free. It's better for them and for society if they have boundaries. It's a safety issue."

If in doubt, don't spout viewpoints. Stick to the facts.

He leaned against the doorframe like I'd exhausted him. "Look, I don't know how he got out. But I'll keep a better eye on him. Will that make you feel better?" His words dripped with derision.

"Aren't you going to go look for him?"

"He'll come back. He always does."

"So this is a common problem?" My voice rose in judgment, my defenses crumbling. Some people should not be allowed to have animal companions. That was all there was to it.

"Look—" He stepped closer, his face hardening.

Chad pulled me back before either Mr. Lennox or I could get the best of each other. "Thank you for your time," Chad mumbled. "We'll be going."

Chad took my hand and pulled me down the steps. I cast one last incredulous look at Mr. Lennox before deciding I had given him too much time already.

"Why'd you do that for?" I mumbled.

"Because I don't want you to be arrested."

"But—"

"Come on, Sierra. Let's go back to your parents' house. They want you there for their rehearsal dinner, remember? Besides, the police are looking into this. I wouldn't worry about it."

Easy for him to say.

We were leaving one worry and entering into another, I realized. I wondered if Chad realized that I was leading him into the lion's den.

CHAPTER 6

When I reached my parents' house, the sun had already begun to set, casting a lovely orange glow over the landscape. Guests chatted as if the bone was long forgotten. In the background, a harpist doled out a delicate melody. The scene seemed so serene and peaceful.

"You're wearing that?" My mom gawked as I walked into the backyard.

I looked down and saw that I had mud caked up the sides of my jeans. I probably smelled like the woods, too, and Chad hadn't fared much better. We might as well have been working in a pigpen for the day.

"I can go change."

She grabbed my arm. "No, if you get cleaned up, you'll miss the whole thing. It's noble that you want to help the police, but sometimes other priorities come first. Now, find your place card and sit. The pork is getting cold."

My mother knew I didn't eat meat. Maybe she was just stressed and had forgotten. That was what I'd blame her outburst on.

I wandered through the crowd until I found a table

with my name on it. Fortunately, Chad's placard was beside mine. Unfortunately, Greg was sitting on the other side.

My ex smiled brightly as I sat down. "Sierra. So lovely to see you here."

I nodded, wishing Chad hadn't detoured inside to use the bathroom. "Greg."

A waitress came and set a plate down in front of me. I frowned when I saw the slab of meat there. If only meat eaters knew what those poor animals went through before making it on the plate.

Greg leaned closer, wiping his mouth with a linen napkin. "I don't eat meat, either. That was all due to your influence, by the way."

"Aw, and I just thought you'd done it to impress me." I'd fully expected him to revert to his natural carnivorous state when we broke up. That had been the case with most of my exes. I hadn't even tried to convert Chad. If he wanted to change, it would be his decision.

"I've grown up a lot since we dated, Sierra."

I'd thought he was pretty grown up when we were dating. He wasn't exactly the kick-his-shoes-off, throw-his-feet-up, and let-loose kind of guy. I'd always known he'd make a responsible husband, father, and employee. I just didn't want to live that kind of cookie-cutter life. I'd thought he'd realized that, too.

I tried to crane my neck and see if Chad was on his way, without appearing too rude. I didn't see him anywhere. I cleared my throat. "Looks like you're doing well for yourself. I mean, *it* looks like you're doing well for yourself." My mom's voice nagged me silently.

Greg nodded, delicately stabbing a green bean. "I like to think so. I joined a practice two months ago. I just purchased a nice starter home on the outskirts of town."

"Starter home, huh?" I couldn't imagine him in a starter home, but maybe even young doctors right out of med school had their share of financial limitations. I lived in a little two-bedroom apartment in a house that was older than my aunt Yori, and there were months when paying the bills was difficult.

He nodded. "That's right. It's only around six thousand square feet, but in a few years I'll purchase a real place."

I gulped. "Only six thousand, huh? That's barely enough room for one person."

His eyes showed no sign that he picked up on the humor in my words. "I know, but this is all a part of my plan. I just take things one step at a time. Honestly, I have everything I want for this phase of my life." He glanced at me, something warm flickering in his gaze. "Well, nearly everything."

I offered a weak smile, knowing just where he was going with this conversation, and I made sure to continue chasing a cherry tomato around my salad plate. "I'm really happy for you, Greg."

"I have to ask. This fellow you brought with you . . . ?"

My stomach churned because I really didn't want to have this conversation. "Chad."

He nodded. "Yes, Chad. Are you two—?"

Just then, someone peeked over the fence. I'd recognize that red bouffant anywhere. It was the neighbor, Mrs. Jericho! "Excuse me, Greg. I'll be right back."

I threw my linen napkin onto my chair and hurried toward her. I stepped through the gate onto the other side of the fence and saw the neighbor hunched down, her face pressed against the fence right by a slit that would give her a view of the party. She startled when she spotted me.

"Dear me, child. You scared me to death." Somehow, she made it sound like I was the one doing something wrong when she was the one both trespassing and spying.

"Can I help you?"

"I just noticed a lot of commotion on the street today. I wanted to make sure everything was okay."

I pondered how much to say and finally settled with "My parents are renewing their vows. This is the rehearsal dinner."

She pursed her lips and narrowed her eyes. "Of course. My invitation must have gotten lost." Disdain trickled from each word.

"However, if you were talking about the police cars

and not the festivities, then you should know that there have been some questionable activities going on in the neighborhood lately."

"Oh? What do you mean?"

I had to choose my words carefully. "I've heard about the copper thefts in this area. Some people think that's a gateway crime that will only lead to bigger problems. You notice anything strange going on around here lately?"

"Should I have?"

"I'm not sure. What can you tell me about the Lennoxes?" I put the bait out there, hoping I'd feel a tug on the line. Instantly, guilt pounded at me because I'd merely *thought* in terms of a fishing analogy. What was happening to me?

"I never even see them home at the same time. It's almost like they're living two separate lives."

"Reggie seems like he has a temper."

She snorted. "To say the least. For the last couple of months, both of them have been so busy yelling at each other that no one wants to be around them. Apparently not even the dog. Finally, they got a dog walker to give the poor pooch some attention."

"For Big Boy?"

She raised a thin eyebrow. "Who?"

"I mean, they hired someone to walk their dog? He's precious."

"I'm not sure if Reggie thinks so. Lately, he's always grumbling as he's throwing him outside. I don't even know why they have a dog. They don't seem like the types."

"Why would they have a dog, then?"

She shrugged. "Status? To prove a point? To attempt to live the American dream?"

What did she mean by that? Maybe the woman was just trying to start trouble.

"Well, I guess I should be getting back to dinner before anyone realizes I'm gone."

"I guess you should. Ta-ta." She tinkled her fingers in the air.

"Ta-ta." Did people actually say that? No one in my circles did, not unless they were making fun of people who did. What I wouldn't give to have Gabby here right now to crack one of her jokes.

I slipped back into the backyard and noticed the catering crew had started cleaning up. Most of my family had gone into the house, except for a few stragglers who were shooting the breeze. The sun was nearly gone now. It was still cold outside, but since I was wearing jeans and a T-shirt, I couldn't feel the frigid temperatures as much.

"Sierra?" a familiar voice said.

My heartbeat softened when I spotted Chad walking toward me.

"I've been looking for you."

"Long story. Did you eat yet?"

"I grabbed a roll and added some barbecue to it. Your aunt Yori grabbed me and talked my ear off about all things anime. Who would have ever thought? Your sister's husband, Mark, rescued me. Nice guy."

I nodded. "He's an anesthesiologist."

"Is everyone in your family in medicine?"

"Essentially." I took his arm. "Let's sit down. Just for a minute."

I just wanted a moment to feel like myself. I wasn't ready to go inside and put up pretenses yet. It exhausted me too much.

"You're never going to forget this visit here, are you?" I cuddled beside him on the swing overlooking the small, kidney-shaped swimming pool.

We were just out of sight of the remaining guests. I could still hear the catering crew clanging dishes and silverware together. Occasionally, Ms. Blankenship's voice rose above the noise as she doled out directions.

"Not in a million years." He squeezed my hand and smiled down on me in a way that still made my stomach do flip-flops.

I put my head on his chest. "Thanks for coming."

"You know I wouldn't miss it. Your family is . . . different than mine."

"I warned you."

"I don't think anything you could have told me would fully prepare me for the force known at the Nakamuras."

I chuckled. "You're probably right."

Just then I heard a bark on the other side of the fence. Chad and I looked at each other. I stood and opened the gate. As soon as I did, Big Boy charged inside and licked my face, nearly knocking me to the ground in the process. I tried to forget about where that mouth had been — mostly, the dead body part — and I couldn't help but giggle at his kisses. Before anyone else saw him, I led him behind the guesthouse and away from any witnesses.

"What are you doing back here?" I asked him, as if he'd answer. He panted and licked my cheeks with enough force to rock me back.

"He must have gotten away from the police."

Chad pulled the dog off me, just enough that I could regain my balance.

"You think?" I rubbed the dog's ears.

"I don't know why else he would be here. Unless he's stalking you."

"Dogs don't stalk. They hunt. I prefer to think Big Boy is admiring me, speaking to me, pleading for my help." My brain started whirling a million miles a minute. "I need to put him somewhere safe until the police come to get him."

"You want to keep him here?" Chad raised an eyebrow.

I nodded, knowing he couldn't really be all that surprised. I had a reputation for going above and beyond for animals. Protesting whaling. Sending nasty letters to fast food chains. Breaking into farms and freeing the livestock before they became someone's next meal.

"You're going to be harboring a fugitive."

"Aren't you overspeaking? I mean, really? Big Boy? A fugitive?"

Chad shrugged, a mischievous glint in his gaze. "Have it your way. But when I go to bail you out, everyone will find out we're secretly married because you'll have to give your real name."

CHAPTER 7

Chad had a point, but I had to think about the bigger picture here. "Can he stay with you tonight in the guesthouse?"

His eyebrows drew back in surprise. "Me? Why me?"

"Because I can't sneak him into the house. Everyone would know. I'll go inside and tell everyone you had a headache and went to bed early. They won't think anything of it. They might even appreciate having me to themselves."

"Or they'll severely dislike me when they figure out what I'm really doing." Chad pressed his lips together and stared at me.

Then I did something I only reserved for emergencies. I gave Chad my puppy-dog eyes. They were my last resort, my act of final desperation. I'd hate myself later for this girlie-girl warfare tactic. "Please, Chad."

"Not that look." He raised a hand to shield himself, blinking as if a blinding light glared in his eyes.

I batted my eyelashes again. "Please?"

"You know I can't resist." He looked away before I

could flutter my eyes again, and he let out a long sigh as he glanced at the guesthouse. "What am I going to do if someone finds the dog out here? What do I say?"

"That I put you up to it. You can totally throw me under the bus. I'm okay with it."

He turned back toward me and slowly nodded. "Okay. But I'm only doing this for you."

I let out a soft squeal and threw my arms around him. "Thank you, thank you, thank you."

Big Boy joined the festivities by barking as well. I quickly shushed him before anyone else could hear and be alerted.

A touch of doubt remained in Chad's eyes. "Are you sure we shouldn't call the police? I'm thinking we should. I don't want this to turn out badly."

"I'll call them in the morning. In the meantime, we'll monitor Big Boy. Any evidence, however stinky, will be handed over immediately."

"Any sweet romantic thoughts I had just disappeared."

"Sorry."

He stared at me a moment, warmth emanating from his gaze. "You should get inside."

I kissed him before pulling away. "Thanks again."

"You can make it up to me later."

***

"Where's Chad?" my mom asked when I joined the

family — and Greg — in the living room.

"He turned in early for the evening. I think he's really tired."

My mother stared at me suspiciously before raising her chin and letting out a stern grunt. "I see. Have a seat and tell us about your life. Your once-every-two-months phone call doesn't paint a complete picture."

My hands were sweating by the time I sat down in the very formal — and did I mention white? — living room. "Nothing too exciting. I was named executive director for Paws and Furballs."

My mother let out another "proper" grunt. I wasn't aware that people were capable of making a grunt sound so formal. "Interesting name for your organization."

"One of the first things I plan on doing next year is changing it. We're still debating the possibilities."

"Have you staged any of those protests lately?" my father asked.

"We were instrumental in exposing the use of deceased whales in the development and production of that new lipstick. We also — "

"Animals were put here on earth for us to use and enjoy, Sierra," my mom interrupted. "I don't understand your obsession. You'd rather humans suffer than beasts?"

My pulse spiked. "No, but I feel there's a balance. I draw the line at cruelty."

"There was so much you could have done with your

life, Sierr—" my mother started, her voice laced with disappointment.

"I think it's great that you're working to better the welfare of animals," Greg added, leaning on his knees toward me, his pupils way too big for my comfort. "It's wonderful that you can find something you're passionate about and make a living at it."

"Sierra's sister helps in a way that's helpful to both animals and humans," my mother stated, her voice softening some.

Score one for Greg. He could do something I'd never been able to accomplish—he could thaw the ice queen.

"Isn't it wonderful that we can all have different roles here on this earth?" Greg continued. He put his hand on my knee and squeezed. "Sierra's doing something she believes in, and she's trying to leave the world a little better than she found it."

I quickly slipped from out of his grasp. Despite the fact that he'd busted a move, I was grateful he was here. He'd helped smooth a rough conversation, and his words had validated me. That didn't happen often here at home.

When no one said anything, I stood. "You know, I'm tired from the drive, and I'd like to get some rest before the ceremony tomorrow. If you'll excuse me, I'm going to turn in for the night."

My stomach turned with nausea again. Must be stress of being here, of the dog, of being sneaky. Lying down truly did sound good.

Before anyone could object, I waved good night and hurried upstairs. My heart was pounding out of control by the time I reached my room, and unshed tears burned in my eyes.

Why did my family always make me feel so small? Why couldn't they understand how fulfilled I felt—except when I was around them?

I fell back on my bed and instinctively reached for one of my old stuffed cats.

Don't think about your family, Sierra. Think about Big Boy instead.

Coping mechanism number one in my life: channel all your frustration into saving animals. It had worked for me in the past and helped me get through some of the lonely days of my childhood. I had to dwell on the things I could control instead of trying to change other people.

I stood and walked to the window. I slid it open, feeling the need for some fresh air. The backyard was dark now, but I had a bird's-eye view of the layout for tomorrow's ceremony.

As I glanced at the guesthouse where Chad was staying, I paused.

Someone was outside the cottage, peering in a window.

No, it couldn't be.

I looked closer. But it was!

Copper thief? Maybe.

But the memory of that bone that Big Boy had brought to me — and the dead body in the woods — and the more logical choice was obvious.

I had to get down there now before someone killed my husband, just like they'd killed Reggie Lennox's wife!

CHAPTER 8

I grabbed the first thing I could find in my room—an old Hello Kitty umbrella—and darted into the hallway. I decided to go the back way, just to ensure that no one would spot me. At least it would decrease the likelihood.

Pretending I was actually good at being stealthy I crept down the hallway, holding the umbrella like a baseball bat. I peered around the stairway and saw that everyone lingered in the living room. Perfect.

I crept through the kitchen, shielded by the island in the center of the room. Remaining low, I reached the back door.

"Sierra?"

I looked up and saw Aunt Yori staring down at me, a bottle in her hand. I put a finger over my mouth, begging for her silence.

She raised the bottle and begged for my silence.

We had an understanding between us. I wouldn't tell anyone she'd been sneaking alcohol, and she wouldn't tell anyone I was sneaking out.

She leaned toward me and whispered a little too loudly, "If I was dating a man who looked like that, I'd pay him some late-night visits, too."

I gulped, hoping no one had heard her. Then I forced a smile, cracked the door open, and snuck outside.

What exactly was I going to do when I ran into this intruder? Knock him over the head with my umbrella? Wouldn't that just be perfect?

Someone who was brutal enough to murder his wife wouldn't bat an eyelash at killing me.

I didn't give up. I remained on the perimeter of my yard, staying in the shadows as I moved closer to the guesthouse. I knew one thing: I couldn't let Chad die. Not on my life.

Big Boy started barked inside the house, and another thought occurred to me: Chad and I were going to be caught red handed with a dog labeled as police evidence.

Of course, we'd be caught if one of us died also.

I needed to ensure neither of those things happened. First priority: saving Chad.

I reached the edge of the house. Where had the shadow gone? Was he inside the house already?

It was country dark out here. Where I lived was close to the city, and it never really got dark, only semi-dark. But out here in the grand suburbs — I called them that because that was what I considered the upper-class suburbs — the dark was almost blinding.

Big Boy barked again, more frantically this time. My heart rate increased as the seriousness of the situation hit me again. This wasn't a child's game of hide-and-seek. There could be real danger, and here I was acting like I had a clue what I was doing.

I lowered my Hello Kitty umbrella, realizing it would do little good. I was confronting a cold-blooded killer. The thought made my blood freeze.

A twig snapped in the distance.

My ears perked as my muscles tightened. As soon as I heard the sound, a scurry of leaves brushed over the lawn.

Had I been hearing things? Was the sound just a part of the wind that swept around me? Or was it tied to something more sinister?

I gripped the flimsy umbrella, at once switching how I held it. The hard plastic kitty head on the handle was the most lethal part. I might need to utilize it.

I reached the corner of the house, and I hadn't seen anyone. Big Boy's barks had lessened. Was that because something had happened to him? Or was all of this overblown, my imagination working overtime?

With a burst of courage, I jetted across the grass and reached the house. I ducked behind a leafy shrub. With a deep gulp of air, I peered around.

There he was! The shadow. He crouched by the window, his face leering inside the house.

I watched as he rose. I still couldn't see his face or tell anything about him, other than he was clearly male. That was based on the set of his shoulders, his flat chest, the way he carried himself.

Was it Mr. Lennox? I couldn't be sure.

He took a step toward the door. His hand reached for the handle.

I couldn't let him get inside. I wouldn't.

With courage I didn't know I had, I raised the umbrella, and together Hello Kitty and I charged toward the intruder.

A guttural cry escaped me, reminiscent of my Amazon ancestors. Only I was Asian. Okay, so I tapped into my inner Mulan.

As the battle cry filled the air, the intruder turned.

Big Boy barked.

A shadow moved across the window.

That's when I clearly saw the man's face.

When I did, all the wind left my lungs.

CHAPTER 9

"Greg?"

He dropped his hand from the door. "Sierra?"

"What are you doing?" I asked, lowering my umbrella.

"I thought I saw someone out here and wanted to make sure everything was okay. I figured it could be someone looking for trouble, at the worst, or Aunt Yori acting foolish, at the least."

I narrowed my eyes. "It looked more like something sinister to me."

The door opened and Chad stood there, looking just as confused as the rest of us. His hair was tousled; he wore his flannel pants and a white undershirt. Had he actually slept through all of that?

"What in the world . . . ?" he muttered.

Big Boy bounded past him and jumped on me, sending my umbrella clattering to the ground. Some protector I was. A fifty-pound dog had just taken me out.

Greg raised his hands, looking back and forth from Chad to me. "I can explain."

"Explain what? Why are both of you outside my

door?"

Greg cringed. I wasn't sure why I felt the need to protect him, but I did. He'd only ever been kind. "Greg thought he saw someone out here, and he feared something might be wrong. Then I saw someone lurking out here, and *I* thought something might be wrong. That brings us to this moment right now."

Greg's shoulders slumped slightly. "That's right. I was just trying to be a good citizen, especially with all the copper thefts around here lately."

Chad's eyes darted back and forth between the two of us. He didn't buy the story, but he remained quiet. "And now here we all are."

Greg pointed to Big Boy, who now sat beside me panting happily. "I thought the police . . ."

I raised a hand. "It's a long story. The less you know, the better."

"Did you guys . . . ? I thought he was in police custody." I could tell Greg was trying to process everything, and each conclusion he drew disturbed him. He looked at me, a huge knot between his eyebrows. "I never took you for a criminal, Sierra."

"I'm not. I—"

A smile tugged at his lips as he perked. "I kind of like this side of you. You've changed."

"What are you—" Chad took a step toward him. He wasn't angry. Chad wasn't the angry type. But he was getting irritated. He sucked in a deep breath and seemed to compose himself. "You do realize I'm standing here, right?"

Greg's expression slipped back into professional mode. "Of course. Sorry about that." He glanced back at me, neutralizing his expression. "Okay, now that I know everything is fine out here, I guess I'll be going."

He took a step away when I called to him. "Greg?"

He paused. "Yes?"

I pointed from Chad to Big Boy to me. "We need to keep this quiet, okay? Please." I hoped he heard the urgency in my voice.

After a moment he nodded, a twinkle dancing in his eyes. "Of course. Anything for you, Sierra."

I watched as he disappeared; then I turned back to Chad. He took my arm and pulled me into the guesthouse like a smuggler on the lookout for custom officials. "What are you doing here?"

"What I said was true. I saw someone out here, and I thought it could be Mr. Lennox coming back to destroy any evidence or possible witnesses in connection to the death of his wife."

Chad stared at me patiently. "Okay, first of all, you came out here with a Hello Kitty umbrella to defend yourself with?"

I shrugged self-consciously. "It was all I could find."

"Secondly, we don't know that body was his wife, nor do we know that he's guilty."

I conceded to his points. "That's true."

"And finally, while I think it's adorable, if you really think a killer is coming after me, please call the police instead of trying to stop him yourself. Okay?"

I nodded. "I didn't have time to think. I just reacted."

He pulled me toward him and kissed my forehead. "I know."

I remained in his embrace for a moment, enjoying the warmth of his arms. "I miss you already."

"We could clear all of this up very easily."

I pulled away, crossed my arms, and frowned. "I know. But—"

He raised a hand to stop me. "You don't have to explain again." Then he turned me toward the door. "But you do have to go. If you want to keep up this charade, then you can't be caught out here. Neither can I, for that matter."

"Not even a kiss?" I asked, looking over my shoulder at him.

"Nope, not even a kiss. It's too risky. So, good night, love. I'll see you in the morning. Your parents have a big day ahead of them tomorrow. And, as has been emphasized several times, nothing can go wrong. Nothing."

***

I was awoken early to the sound of the doorbell ringing.

I lay in bed a moment, uncertain that I'd heard correctly.

Another *dong* rang out. It was definitely a doorbell.

How late had I slept? My alarm must not have gone off like it was supposed to.

Unwillingly, I pulled an eye open. The clock beside my nightstand read 6:30.

Who in the world would ring the doorbell this early?

Voices drifted up from downstairs, and something in my subconscious knew trouble was brewing. Quickly, I threw my clothes on, raked a hand through my hair, and scrambled toward the noise.

I stopped in my tracks when I saw Detective Meadows in the doorway talking with my mom and dad. Her grim expression matched the dreary gray suit she wore.

Nothing can go wrong today echoed in my mind.

With a start like this, I had a feeling that everything would go wrong.

I joined the crowd—which included Reina and Aunt Yori—with a touch of trepidation racing through me. I knew whatever was being said couldn't be good.

"The dog went missing from custody, and we're wondering if anyone here has seen him?" the detective said.

"The case of the missing dog," Aunt Yori whispered, mischief in her voice.

"Why would we have seen him?" my dad asked.

I'd bet anything his eyebrow was twitching.

"We're scouring the neighborhood in case he ran

back in the direction of his home," Detective Meadows said.

"So you came back here at this hour of the morning to ask? Couldn't it wait until later? A more reasonable hour?" My mother yanked her housecoat closer.

"In a murder investigation, every minute counts," the detective countered.

"The dog was murdered?" Aunt Yori asked.

"No, the dog found a dead body," I corrected. "Speaking of which, how'd the dog get away?"

Everyone turned, finally noticing I was there.

"He slipped away from his handler when we tried to take him out of the cruiser at animal control," Detective Meadows said.

"Can you blame him for wanting to get away?" I asked in the poor dog's defense.

"Sierra!" My mother's eyes were wide with embarrassment.

Obviously, I needed to explain myself. "While I can appreciate animal shelters in some regards, in other ways they're—"

"Enough." My mom stared me down, her tone leaving no room for argument.

Detective Meadows eyed me, a new glint in her gaze. "I understand you're an animal rights activist."

My throat went dry as the meaning of her words spread through me like the aftermath of an atomic bomb. "You checked me out."

"Standard procedure in a case like this," she said.

But I knew better. I'd been the one who called the police at the Lennoxes', the dog had come to me last night when he escaped from his home again, and I'd been there when they'd found the body. I was on law enforcement's radar now.

"Do you mind if we check out your house and property?" Detective Meadows turned back to my parents.

All my muscles tightened as anxiety zipped through me. This wasn't good. It wasn't good at all.

"Of course," my father said. "We have nothing to hide."

"I did sneak in a few cigarettes. Don't tell Mai, okay?" Aunt Yori said a little too loudly.

So much for not ruining their big day. They were going to be furious with me when they found Big Boy in their guesthouse.

Officers invaded the home. There were four of them, and they spread out to look for the canine, scattering like fleas searching for a new homestead on a pound puppy.

"Those are some fine-looking men in uniform," Aunt Yori continued, staring after the police officers and nodding her head in approval.

I could do nothing but stand there. If I made a run for the guesthouse, everyone would know something was up. The best thing would be to remain calm and not raise suspicions.

But Chad . . .

I'd pulled Chad into the middle of this, and now he could face consequences that I could hardly bear to think about. Maybe I should just come clean now? I could fess up to my role in all of this and clear Chad before this went any further.

My blood seemed to buzz as I considered my options. I really didn't have many options, did I? I had to make things right.

I knew Chad. He'd defend me. He'd say it was his idea. He would be the one who got in trouble.

I couldn't let that happen.

I needed to fess up. Now.

I cleared my throat, feeling like I might throw up again. "Excuse me? Detective Meadows? There's something I need to tell you."

CHAPTER 10

"Good morning, everyone. What's going on?"

My eyes widened when I spotted Chad behind me. He stretched, still wearing his PJs and hair messy like he'd been woken from a deep slumber. He grasped a cup of coffee in one hand and had come from the direction of the kitchen.

I stared at him, trying to piece together what was happening.

Why was he in the house? Where was Big Boy? Exactly what was going on?

Detective Meadows explained things to Chad. He nodded like all of this was a surprise and then took a sip of his coffee, not appearing the least bit ruffled.

"Lots of excitement around here," he finally mumbled. He stole a quick glance at me.

The detective turned back to me. "You were about to say something?"

That's right. I'd been ready to implicate myself. I had to improvise, and quickly. I rubbed my throat. "I thought you should know that when I was outside of Reggie Lennox's house yesterday, I saw what appeared to be a bloody tarp in his backyard."

"You were snooping at his house?" She twisted her head ever so slightly to let me know she thought my actions were odd.

That was her reaction to what I'd said? Really? What about the evidence? "I went back to his house to pick up my leash that I left earlier."

She continued to eye me suspiciously. "And where was this tarp?"

"In a wheelbarrow in his backyard behind the shed."

"Is there a reason you keep pulling Mr. Lennox into this?" Her steely gaze welded onto mine.

I shook my head. "Why would I?"

"Maybe because he just took over as CEO of the largest fur coat company on the East Coast?"

My mouth dropped open. "What?"

She nodded, looking a little too pleased with herself. "It's true."

"If that was the case, I'd hurt Reggie, not his wife."

My mother gasped. "Sierra!"

I shrugged quickly and stepped back. "I mean, I didn't hurt anyone. But think this through. The pieces don't fit together when you examine possible motives. Besides, I had no idea what the Lennoxes' backgrounds were until you just told me."

My mom's mouth dropped open. This was not one of her proud maternal moments, and I regretted that. But I'd spoken the truth, like it or not.

"I didn't get to town until yesterday evening," I

continued. "That body appeared older than that."

"I'd say it was there at least two days," Chad added with a shrug. "That's based purely on my background as a mortician."

"She's got a point," Detective Meadows conceded, nibbling on her bottom lip a moment.

Relief filled me. I hadn't been the captain of my debate team for nothing.

Then the detective's death stare reappeared. "But we're still searching the residence."

The relief disappeared just as fast as it had materialized.

I stood there, desperately wanting to talk to Chad, to figure out where Big Boy was and what had happened. I had to plan wisely, though. One wrong look, one ill-timed whispered conversation, and I could be an even bigger target on the detective's radar.

An officer poked his head in through the back door. "Detective, I think you'll want to see this."

Chad and I exchanged a glance. This wasn't good. I was already picturing dog hair, muddy paw prints, and a big, dopey Big Boy watching from the window of the guesthouse.

Since my mom and dad began to follow everyone to the backyard, Chad and I found ourselves swept into the current as well.

I tried to brace myself for the oncoming wave of bad news.

***

"There's no sign the dog is still here," the officer said as we all joined him by the fence. "But there are paw prints here in the mud by the gate."

My gaze met Chad's. Where in the world was Big Boy? While I was relieved I hadn't been caught red handed, my next thought had gone to the dog and his safety.

"Those could have been left yesterday, Officer Hawkins." The detective glared at the impressions in the soft dirt in front of her.

Clearly, they were from a dog. But they didn't really tell the police anything they didn't already know. Thank goodness.

Finally, after what felt like hours of standing and fidgeting and watching everyone do their jobs, Detective Meadows turned to us. "Thank you for your compliance. I'm sorry to have disturbed you. You'll be around if we have any more questions?"

"Of course. I hope you find Big Boy soon," I said.

The detective didn't smile when she looked back at me. "I do, too."

As soon as everyone scattered, I turned to Chad. We remained outside in the brisk morning air. The edges of my flannel pants were wet from the dew on the grass, but I didn't care. "What happened?"

"I saw the police outside the house this morning. I opened the door to find out what was going on, and

Big Boy ran out. Again."

"Where did he go?"

"He jumped over the fence and disappeared into the woods. I started to go after him, but he was gone. It's obvious that dog is going to do whatever he wants to do. Then things started clicking in my mind, and I figured I better clean up. I ran the vacuum and washed the dog bowls. Thankfully."

I nodded in total agreement. "If the police had found those things . . ."

"I would be their prime suspect."

I didn't like the sound of that, and it wasn't totally accurate. "I actually think I'm on their radar. Apparently Mr. Lennox owns a fur company. Detective Meadows did research on me and knows about my opposition to careers such as that."

"Did you know about the fur company?"

"Of course I didn't know that!" My voice rose to an abnormally high pitch.

Chad glanced around. "Keep calm."

"What are we going to do?"

Chad leaned closer, his eyes unblinking and serious. "Leave it to the police."

"But . . ."

"Not buts about it."

"The *nerve* of some people!" someone screeched in the distance.

I glanced over and couldn't believe my eyes. "Mom?"

She stormed out the back door, my dad right behind her. She stopped at the deck railing, staring across the backyard and reminding me of Scarlett O'Hara on her balcony, realizing all was lost.

My normally put-together mom would never act like this if she were in her right mind.

That meant whatever happened really must be bad.

I strode across the grass toward her. "What's wrong?"

"That woman," she seethed, flipping her head back to indicate someone behind her.

"The detective?" I was usually good at assuming things, but not so much in this case. She could be referring to Aunt Yori saying something inappropriate, Ms. Blankenship missing a cobweb, Sharo forgetting if rings or "I do" came first in the ceremony.

Her eyes narrowed. "No. Mrs. Jericho."

Not who I'd expected. "What about her?"

"She's having a yard sale. A yard sale! Today of all days." For my mom, this was apparently a North-defeating-the-South moment. Or, in my family's case, the West outdoing the East.

"What's so bad about a yard sale?" I asked, realizing I was probably opening a can of worms—a saying I was totally opposed to, in case anyone asked.

Her eyes went crazy wide. She and Aunt Yori were definitely related; I'd just never seen the resemblance before.

"A yard sale? Today? The street will be flooded

with traffic now, and my guests will have nowhere to park. She did this on purpose."

"She flooded the street with traffic?" I clarified.

"Precisely!" My mom raised her index finger in the air. "That's what kind of woman she is. K.T., go see if she has a permit. If she doesn't, the police can shut her down. You have to have a permit in this area."

"Yes, Mai." My dad knew better than to argue. None of us had ever seen my mom in her bridezilla state. Well, maybe my dad had, but I couldn't even imagine the two of them ever being young, foolish, and in love. Like, not at all. Not even if I closed my eyes and tried really, really hard.

My mom, still in a tizzy, turned on her heel.

"And for goodness' sakes, you two. Put some real clothes on."

I glanced down at my modest PJs and frowned. It wasn't like I would have worn these outside if I hadn't been summoned out of bed by the police. I didn't bother to argue, though.

Mother stomped toward the house. My sister threw a disparaging glance over her shoulder at me and hurried after Mom.

"I've never seen her like that," someone muttered beside me. Based on the shrill voice, it wasn't Chad.

I glanced over and saw the wedding planner. Where had she come from? Last I'd heard, she was one of the few people associated with the ceremony who wasn't spending the night here.

"Your parents have been obsessing over this day for months, you know. It's a shame things appear to be going wrong right now."

"Really? Because I just heard about it two weeks ago." Funny how that had worked out.

"She's been going a little crazy, if you know what I mean," Sharo muttered, examining one of her red fingernails while clutching a clipboard.

"No, actually I don't." What was she talking about?

"She's just been very uptight. Very obsessed with crossing every *t* and dotting every *i*, you know?"

I nodded. I supposed I could understand. Chad and I had run away and eloped, so I couldn't fully appreciate how stressful a formal ceremony might be. Nor could I understand why my mom, who never seemed like the sentimental type, was so obsessed with renewing her vows. But to each their own . . . unless it came to mistreating animals.

Sharo held her clipboard out, and I caught a quick glance and saw some numbers there: 41. 25. 38.

What were they for? Seating arrangements of some sort? An itemized bill? I had no idea.

She noticed me looking and held the papers closer. "I only hope that dog doesn't show up again."

"Why?"

"Because then everything really will be ruined."

Somehow in the process of all of this, people had lost sight of the fact that the real tragedy here was that a human life had been lost. A ruined ceremony paled in comparison, but I had a feeling I wouldn't convince anyone else of that.

CHAPTER 11

Chad and I had gone into our rooms, respectively, and gotten ready.

By the time we got back downstairs, my dad had come back and informed everyone that the evil Mrs. Jericho had a permit and wouldn't back down. She was having that sale whether we liked it or not, and it was her God-given right as a citizen of this town.

My mom let out another inhuman screech, and that's when I knew I had to do something.

"Let me go talk to her," I said.

Chad looked at me like I was crazy.

So did everyone else, for that matter.

I shrugged, slightly offended. "What? I'm a great negotiator."

Everyone continued to stare in disbelief.

"I am," I insisted, not losing any of my gusto.

Moments flashed back in my mind. Images where I'd failed terribly at negotiating. Scenarios where I'd protested certain events while wearing tiger costumes and sitting in cages for all the world to see.

Maybe *negotiator* wasn't the best word. But I could be provocative and challenging.

"I'm going," I said firmly, not one to be easily discouraged. I was nothing if not tenacious.

"I'm going with her," Chad said, casting me another incredulous look.

We slipped outside, the sunlight now warming the air a little bit more. Chad fell into step beside me as we walked down the driveway. Silence stretched between us, the only sounds that of the birds tweeting and the faint murmur of a crowd in the distance.

"You really think you're going to talk her out of this yard sale?" Chad asked when we reached the sidewalk.

I shook my head, trying to tamp down the bounce in my step. I loved a good challenge. "No, not at all."

"Then what are you up to?"

"What makes you think I'm up to something? A walk sounded good, you know?"

"Uh-huh," Chad mumbled.

The yard sale certainly was in full swing. Sure, we had yard sales all the time back home. But this yard sale seemed different. It was . . . busy, for starters. Like, really busy. There must have been twelve cars lined up down the road. I could hear the crowd from several yards away. And I even heard a . . . bullhorn?

As we rounded the patch of trees, I spotted Mrs. Jericho standing in the middle of rows and rows of neatly organized tables. And, sure enough, she had a bullhorn to her lips. "I've got china here that's worth five hundred dollars, and I'm only asking one hundred. It's a steal of a deal. Don't let this one pass you by."

What was this? An auction? Or did Mrs. Jericho really know how to run a sale? I'd never seen anything like it.

"Let's split up. Less intimidating that way," I suggested.

He nodded and made his way toward a table of tools.

I squeezed between a display of collectible stuffed animals and another filled with creepy-looking dolls. I inched closer to my parents' eccentric neighbor, who continued to talk at a rapid pace on that bullhorn, even going as far as to stand on an old dining room chair.

People *loved* it. They were practically throwing money at her. She had some kind of apron around her waist with a change dispenser, a pocket for paper bills, and a place where she even swiped credit cards.

I picked up a piece of Tupperware and waited for a good break or even for her to take a breath, for that matter.

It didn't come. She kept chattering on and on.

Finally, I backed away, my ears ringing and a headache beginning.

"She knows how to run a yard sale, doesn't she?" another woman said as she riffled through some hardback books.

"You can say that again."

"I'm not usually a yard sale person, but I just couldn't resist coming over here to see what she had. Mrs. Jericho always knows how to keep things interesting here on the street."

I perked. "You live on this street?"

She nodded. "Sure do. For now, at least. We're hoping to upgrade in the near future."

Upgrade? As if these houses weren't large enough. It wasn't my place to say that. Not everyone was content with minimalist lifestyle choices. "Less is more" had sustained me many days.

I glanced at the woman more closely. She was probably in her forties. Though she was thin, she had big bones and dark hair cut in a short bob, and she wore expensive-looking jeans along with a black sweater.

Maybe she could add some insights to what was going on around here, starting with the body found in the woods last night. So far she seemed in the know.

"Is this street always so exciting?" I asked casually.

"You mean the woman they found dead yesterday?" The lady leaned closer. "I couldn't believe it either. The police have been all over this neighborhood since then. I find it hard to believe that anyone on this street would have anything to do with it. I hate to even think about it."

"Did the cops find anything?" I asked, glancing around to make sure no one else was listening.

She shrugged, holding up an old Agatha Christie hardback and skimming the back cover. "I'm not sure. I do know they took a tarp. Said there was blood on it."

I straightened, electricity zinging through me.

Detective Meadows had been listening!

"Whose blood do you think it was?" I continued, pretending to be interested in the ugliest plaid skirt I'd ever laid eyes on.

"It was stain. Just red stain from the deck." She put the book back onto the table and moved on to a Sue Grafton paperback.

"Are you sure?"

The woman paused. "Sure about what?"

"About the stain?" I leaned closer again. "That Mr. Lennox, do you think he could have . . . ?"

The woman scrunched her eyebrows together. "Could have what?"

I shrugged, trying to look casual. "I don't know. Offed his wife, maybe?"

She jerked back, her eyes widening. "Why in the world would you ask that?"

I needed to rethink this plan because several people were glancing over now, questions in their eyes as the emotion filling the woman's words intensified. "Because she hasn't been seen in days."

"That's because I was out of town with work!"

I gulped, not liking the conclusions I was drawing. "What?"

"That's right. I'm Mrs. Lennox, and I resent your implications!"

CHAPTER 12

Most people would have been embarrassed enough to leave at that point. Not me. I made a living by drawing attention to myself. But I only did when the situation warranted it.

That meant that even though people were doing the suburban equivalent of shunning me, I stayed around anyway.

"I thought you were out of town until next week?" I continued.

She scowled. "I came back early."

With that, she stormed away, not only from me but from the entire yard sale.

Chad joined me, questions in his gaze. "What did you do?"

"I just offended someone. Nothing new."

He looked unfazed. "Did you talk to Mrs. Jericho yet?"

I shook my head, glancing over at her. "No, she won't stop living out her secret childhood fantasy of being an auctioneer. Her voice is going to haunt me in my sleep. I'm convinced of it."

"What now?"

"Give me just a few more minutes. I'm not ready to give up yet."

I continued to scout out the yard sale. Every once in a while, I would scan my environment. Part of me hoped to see Big Boy come galloping through again, just as he'd done last night. But, so far he hadn't made an appearance.

In the distance, Mrs. Jericho continued her bid for saleswoman of the year, and neighbors were clamoring to buy things. More cars had pulled up, and people seemed to be feeding on the frenzy of other customers. They were snatching up things left and right.

"I heard what you said back there." A frumpy, fifty-something blonde approached me at the baby-clothing table.

Baby clothing? I needed to get away from these before the rumors started.

The woman continued, talking low so no one else could hear. "Those two do have a lot of problems. Don't let anyone tell you differently."

"You mean, the Lennoxes?" I clarified.

She nodded. "Yes, the Lennoxes. I go on a walk every morning. I've heard them arguing before. I can hear it all the way out on the street."

"Wow, must be some fights they're having."

"Thank goodness they don't have any kids. It's bad enough their dog is in the middle of this."

My heart panged at the thought of Big Boy. "Poor dog."

She nodded. "I know. The dog walker gave him more attention than anyone else."

At least they'd been kind enough to hire someone to do what they should have done. I'd give them credit for that. Like kids, canines needed TLC too.

I wondered if Mr. Lennox ever thought about skinning that poor dog so his wife could wear him around her pretty little neck.

I shook my head. No. This was not *101 Dalmatians* playing out in real life. I couldn't bear to think about it. The idea was too absurd. Stuff like that didn't happen in reality . . . but what if it did?

"So, you saw the dog on your walks?"

The woman nodded. "Seven a.m. every morning, just like clockwork." She suddenly frowned. "Until three days ago. They must have fired her. It's a shame, but I hear that family is very hard to please. I guess it's no surprise, not in that sense."

I chewed on those words. Was it important? I couldn't be sure. But it was something to think about.

***

I walked back into my parents' house and instantly felt my entire body tense again.

My parents were both waiting for me at the breakfast nook. My mom sipped some coffee while my dad fed their goldfish — the only animals they'd allow to live inside their home, they'd said many times.

"Well?" my mom asked.

I shook my head. "I'm sorry. I wasn't able to talk Mrs. Jericho out of the yard sale."

I'd finally had face time with her, but she'd used that moment to laugh outright and belittle my request on the bullhorn for everyone to hear. It hadn't been all that pleasant, truth be told, but I'd been through worse. I could only conclude that Mrs. Jericho was a very lonely, very sad woman who poured herself into her career.

"She was adamant about the sale," I continued.

And there was something about the gleam in her eyes that told me Mrs. Jericho had chosen this date on purpose. Did she want to ruin my parents' big day? My guess would be yes.

My father put his arm around my mom's shoulders. "It will be fine," he insisted. "The yard sale will be long over before the ceremony tonight."

She nodded with absolutely no conviction and stood. As she hurried upstairs, my father followed behind, trying to console her. It was kind of cute, actually, and I'd never thought of my parents as cute before. The thought threw me off balance for a minute.

Reina came over as soon as my parents were out of earshot. "I watched the news this morning," she started. "There was a report on the body."

"And?" My pulse spiked.

"The medical examiner is saying that it's of a young woman in her early twenties, probably five feet tall, and white."

My mind raced through what I'd just learned at the yard sale. Could this be the answer I was looking for?

"What's wrong, Sierra?"

I shook my head. "I've got to go back to that yard sale. Cover for me!"

"I'm going too," Chad said, right on my heels.

I didn't argue.

CHAPTER 13

"What are you doing?" Chad asked, trying to keep up with me.

I was walking as fast as some of the enthusiastic senior citizens in the mall did every Monday, Wednesday, and Friday morning. If I put more hip and elbow action into it, I might become a certified speed walker. Add a velour sweat suit and I'd be in business.

"There was a lady at the yard sale. She was telling me about a dog walker that she hasn't seen in a few days."

"And you think that's who the dead body is?"

I nodded. "I do. That's why Big Boy had such a loyal reaction. It makes sense."

"I don't know what to say."

"Don't say anything. Just follow my lead."

I stopped at the yard sale, slightly out of breath from the fast walking—which surprised me and made me vow to sign up for aerobics or something. My gaze scanned the crowd, and finally I spotted the woman. She was climbing into her Volvo station wagon.

In a move that probably made me seem on par with my mom when it came to looking like a madwoman, I waved my arms and ran toward her.

She froze, her eyes widening as she seemed to consider whether or not I might hurt her, and then she backed up, shielding herself with her open car door. "Yes?"

If I'd really been a crazy woman, then her best bet would have been to climb in the car and lock the doors. Thankfully, she seemed to value courtesy over safety. It worked in my favor at the moment.

"That dog walker you mentioned?" I started, sucking in another gulp of air.

"Yes?" She still squeezed the door, and her eyes had a frantic look about them.

"What did she look like?"

With measured movements she shook her head. "I don't know. Youngish. Probably in college. Blonde hair. Thin."

"How tall?"

She shrugged. "Kind of short. Maybe a couple of inches shorter than me. I'm five four."

Dread settled in my stomach.

The dog walker fit the description of the body found yesterday.

Now I just needed to figure out how to break that news to the police without incriminating myself.

***

Detective Meadows met me in my parents'

driveway. I really didn't want to upset my folks any more than they already were today. I prayed that my sister had thought of some great excuse as to why I wasn't inside the house right now, some kind of conversational sleight-of-hand trick.

"So you're telling me you think the dead woman is the dog walker?" the detective repeated. She stared at me, that same skeptical, distant look in her eyes.

"That's right. One of the neighbors—" I glanced down at the paper in my hands where I'd scribbled her name. She wouldn't give me her address. At least she'd been that smart. "A Mrs. Linda Goodgame said that she walks the neighborhood every day at seven. She sees a girl walking Big Boy."

"Who's this Big Boy?" The detective shifted her weight from one foot to the other, still looking confused.

I wanted to growl. "The dog! I nicknamed him Big Boy. It's no big deal. I just couldn't call him *mutt*, though. Maybe John Dog . . . you know, instead of John Doe."

The detective didn't look amused. "I get it," she deadpanned.

I straightened. "That's not really important here, though."

"So what makes you think the body we found is the dog walker?"

"Mrs. Goodgame hasn't seen the dog walker in three days. That fits in with the timeline of her death."

The detective shifted as if I'd made her uncomfortable. "How do you know that? We haven't released that information to the press."

I was right? Yes. I loved being right. "It was obvious she hadn't been dead that long! It doesn't take a detective to figure that out!"

"Sierra," Chad whispered, warning in his voice.

I know, I know. I need to watch my tone. Sometimes I got a bit fired up, though. This was one of those times.

"Will you just check her out? Please? I'm trying to stay out of this. I really am. But when clues keep smacking me in the face, what am I supposed to do?"

"If it makes you feel better, I'll talk to the Lennoxes and see what's going on. Okay?" Detective Meadows conceded.

I nodded, resisting the urge to beg her to find Big Boy while she was at it. That poor dog. I hoped he wasn't scared and all alone out there.

Then I remembered Big Boy and his essence. He wasn't the scared kind of dog. He was a take-life-by-the-horns type of canine. He'd come back when he was ready.

As soon as the police pulled away, Sharo pulled up in a cute little Mercedes and came sauntering down the driveway toward me. I noted the mud on her tires. She didn't seem like the muddy-tires kind of lady.

"Is everything all right?" she asked.

"Of course." I nodded toward her car. "Doing some off-roading?"

Her cheeks flushed. "I had to park in the gravel parking lot at the bakery, if you must know."

One of the many hazards of being a wedding planner, I supposed.

"Don't forget—your parents are counting on you today, Sierra." With that, Sharo sashayed inside.

I nodded, guilt flashing through me. I'd let them down in nearly every way—personally, professionally, financially. I supposed I could make a little more effort today.

Before I could plan my next move, my sister and mom stepped outside, designer purses looped on their arms. "It's time for manis and pedis," Reina said. "Let's get going."

I stole a glance at Chad. Manis and pedis? With my mom and sister? I was going to need a lot of prayer to get through this.

CHAPTER 14

"So, tell me about this Chad," my mom said while her toes gurgled in a bath of bubbling water.

My mother, sister, and I all sat in a row in the upscale salon where soothing instrumental music crooned overhead. The floors were marble, the style simplistic, and the workers all dressed in jeans with black T-shirts. This wasn't my scene, but I could be a team player.

I resisted another "owie" remark. The technician was having a field day on my toes. Certainly my cuticles weren't this bad. It wasn't like I didn't groom myself or something.

I braced myself before launching into the conversation about Chad. "He's . . . what can I say? He's great, Mom. I think you'll really like him when you get to know him."

"He's a mortician?" She turned the page in her medical journal. Most women read *Vogue* at places like this. Maybe even *Better Homes and Gardens* or *People*. But not my mom.

I wasn't much better. If I'd had my choice, I'd be reading the new vegan cookbook I'd just purchased.

I exchanged a glance with my sister. The way her eyes grew to owl-like proportions made it clear how she felt this conversation would go.

"He *was* a mortician," I corrected.

"What does he do now?" My mom peered at me over the top of the professional journal.

"He's actually . . ." How did I say this? Why did I care? I was proud of Chad and the work he did. I just didn't want a confrontation with my mom. "He's a crime scene cleaner."

My mom sucked in air so fast she nearly snorted. "A crime scene cleaner, you said?"

I nodded, cringing again as the pedicurist dug into my toenails again. "That's right. He comes in after the police leave and cleans up any hazardous material, among other things. It's a valuable job, and unfortunately, it's necessary to our society today."

"And this is the man you brought home to me?"

I might as well have said he was an escaped convict.

I nodded, refusing to break my gaze with her. "That's correct."

"How would he ever support you, if you were to get married? You can't plan a future based on a career like that."

"His job is decent, Mother. Plus, I work."

"Your job doesn't pay much either, Sierra. Greg, on the other hand, he's really made something of himself."

"Mom . . ." I suddenly felt like a teenager again. No one could exasperate me more quickly than my parents.

"Don't 'Mom' me, Sierra. I've been around the block a few times. You have to think these things through."

Sure she had. She'd been around the block in her luxury BMW. Don't get me wrong — my mom had worked hard to become a doctor. Though I was born of her loins — gross! — I still felt like the two of us came from two totally different worlds.

My sister nodded toward me. I knew what she was implying. She wanted me to tell Mom I was married. I just couldn't do that. Not in good conscience, at least. I needed to spare the workers here from seeing World War III explode before their eyes.

"Just give him a chance. He's a good man," I finally said.

My mom harrumphed and turned back to her reading, her disapproval evident.

I cleared my throat, ready to change the subject. "So, your neighbor, Mrs. Jericho. She's a piece of work."

My mom raised her chin, not bothering to look at me. "She's never liked us."

I peered over her shoulder and saw she was more engrossed in an article about toe fungus than she was in this conversation. "Why is that?"

My mom shrugged a shoulder. "I have no idea why someone wouldn't like us. We're decent humans who add to society. There's nothing not to like."

I begged to differ but knew better than to say so.

The nail tech shook a bottle of cotton-candy-pink nail polish and began twisting the top off. I pulled my feet away from her. For reasons that went beyond aesthetic, I hadn't planned on actually getting my toes painted. "Wait!"

The pedicurist stared at me but said nothing.

"Is that product tested on animals?" I asked.

She continued to stare. Slowly, she shrugged and shook her head. "Am I supposed to know that?"

"Both pearl essence and shimmer come from herring scales—"

Before I could finish, she put the first coat of pink on my toes. I started to argue, to launch into another speech, but I got a warning glance from my mom and sucked it up.

"What does she do for a living?" I continued, trying to keep my mind off the nail polish.

My mom frowned again. "I believe Mrs. Jericho is in sales."

I should have guessed that.

"How about the Lennoxes? What's your feel on them?" The conversation topic seemed safe enough to me.

With a sharp snap, she put her magazine down and looked at me with disdain. "I don't have a feel, Sierra. I only have facts. Feelings deceive."

"What do you know about them, then?" I had to work really hard to keep the edge out of my voice. Besides, anyone else would have given up by now, but not me. My mom was already mad. I'd reached the edge of the cliff and gone over. There was nowhere to go now but down, so I might as well make the most of my free fall.

"They have little time to socialize. She loves fur. They need to cut their grass more. That's about all I know."

I nodded. "Okay, then."

I couldn't believe my good fortune because, lo and behold, who walked into the salon at that moment?

Mrs. Jericho.

There were some good things about living in a small town.

My mom sneered as soon as she spotted her neighbor. "Did your nails get broken in all the hustle of the yard sale?"

Mrs. Jericho sneered back. "No need to be resentful, Mai. I'm just trying to purge my house of extra junk. Nothing wrong with that."

"Close down so early?"

Mrs. Jericho took her place in the chair next to me. "I reached my goal, sold most of my things, and even had time to make my standing appointment here. Every Saturday at noon. Wouldn't miss it for the world."

"Your nails are looking kind of shabby, Mrs. Jericho," the young technician said.

Mrs. Jericho jerked her hand back. "I've been working hard. What can I say?"

I glanced over and saw the dirt underneath her fingernail tips. Interesting. She just didn't strike me as the get-dirty type of woman. No, she struck me as the nosy, let-me-make-life-difficult-for-everyone-around-me type of person.

My mom and sister started talking, and I couldn't bring myself to join in the conversation about changes in insurance plans. Maybe my sister understood that language, but I didn't. Instead, I turned to Mrs. Jericho.

"Look, I know we got started off on the wrong foot. I'm sorry about that."

She said nothing.

I lowered my voice. "I'm worried about my parents now that they're getting older. And then the body that was found behind their house? That's really concerned me. Is this area safe?"

"I've always felt safe here."

"Anyone suspicious around lately? Or anyone out of the ordinary?'

She finally glanced at me. "Why are you asking about this again? We had this conversation last night."

"The best protection against crime is a nosy neighbor. Don't you think?"

That seemed to hit home with her, because the corners of her lips curled ever so slightly. "I do subscribe to that theory."

"I heard something about a dog walker. You ever have any encounters with her?"

"Winnie? I talked to her a couple of times."

I had a name!

"She seemed like a nice girl. If I had a dog, I might have hired her," she continued.

"I heard the Lennoxes fired her."

Her eyes widened. "I did hear some arguments at the house. I had no idea they fired her, though."

I shrugged. "That's just what I heard. You know Winnie's last name? I'm thinking about doing some dog walking on the side. She might have some pointers for me."

She reached into her purse. "As a matter of fact, I have her card. She was trying to drum up some business. It's Winnie Dubois."

Bingo!

My hideous pink toenails were still drying, but I had to slip away for a moment. This couldn't wait. Flexing my toes in the air, I stood.

"What are you doing?" my mom asked.

"I've got to run to the bathroom," I blurted.

"You can't go in there barefoot."

"But I've got to go!" I insisted.

The technician rushed toward me and began trying to slip some flimsy flip-flops on me. I squirmed uncomfortably, trying to keep up the façade that I needed to go potty. Finally, the disposable shoes were on my feet, and I trotted toward the bathroom in the back.

As soon as I closed and locked the door, I pulled my cell phone from my back pocket, opened the Internet browser, and typed in Winnie's name. In a morbid way, I was delighted to see pages of results pop up.

She'd done a good job advertising her dog-walking business and had included contact information. Her name even appeared on a college club website. She'd hosted an event at her place, and it included an address. I knew what I had to do before I went back home tomorrow.

I had to do this for Big Boy's sake. For my parents, even. Once this whole investigation was cleared up, then nothing would ruin their big day.

Just then, someone pounded on the door.

"Sierra, are you okay?" Reina's voice reached through the walls.

I shoved my phone back into my pocket. "Just fine. Coming!"

CHAPTER 15

I attempted to wave goodbye to Mrs. Jericho as I left, but her gaze was fixated on her electronic tablet and she didn't bother to look up. As I walked through the parking lot, I glanced down at the car parked closest to the front door. I recognized it as Mrs. Jericho's. It was hard to miss the bright green Beetle.

I paused at the front fender. A large indention deformed the metal there. How had that happened? It was probably nothing, but Mrs. Jericho didn't seem like the type who'd drive around with a less-than-perfect vehicle.

My sister followed my gaze. "Yep, that's Mrs. Jericho's car. I'd recognize it anywhere. You'll never believe this. I saw her having her car detailed at Max's Wax a couple of days ago. It's located right beside my vet office, and I couldn't help but notice the lime-green paint. It's hard to miss."

"What's so strange about that?" I questioned.

"Mrs. Jericho is a first-class kind of lady. The vet's office where I work is in a not-so-nice part of town. It doesn't make sense that she would drive all the way out there when there are at least two places right here in town that she could have used."

I stored that information away. It was interesting. Had she just happened to be in that part of town? Or was there another reason? My sister was right — Mrs. Jericho didn't seem like the type who'd "stoop as low" as to use a second-rate business to attend to matters.

It could be nothing.

Or it could be everything.

We climbed into the car, my thoughts still turning. If it was Winnie who'd been found behind my parents' property, how had she ended up there? Had the Lennoxes become angry with her? Had she walked in and discovered some kind of illegal activity going on at their place?

What if the Lennoxes weren't connected at all? Maybe Winnie had stumbled across a psycho on one of her morning walks. Maybe she'd been at the wrong place at the wrong time.

As we started down the road, my mom announced that we had to pick up some flowers at the florist and pick up some boxes at her office for the ceremony tonight.

That's when I had an idea.

"Why don't you let me do your errands for you?" I offered.

My mom turned to glance at me. "Really?"

"Yes, really. That will give you some time to go home and get ready for tonight. I know you have a lot to do."

"That's very kind of you, Sierra." My mom sounded surprised.

I was about to defend myself when guilt pressed on me. My intentions *weren't* totally pure. This was no time to confess, though.

I'd drop my mom and sister off, pick up Chad, and then veer off from my errands for long enough to go by Winnie's apartment. If nothing else, my curiosity would be satisfied.

As we continued down the road, something splattered against the windshield. My gaze snapped toward the sound.

Rain. It was starting to rain.

For my mom, this was the equivalent of a tornado crashing through town.

Rain would ruin the whole ceremony, which was planned to be entirely outdoors.

"It's going to pass," my sister muttered, her hands gripping the wheel. The corner of her lips pulled down in a slight frown, though.

My mom said nothing, which in some ways was worse than one of her rants.

This was important to my mom, I realized. I knew people had been saying that repeatedly since I'd been here in Connecticut, but looking at my mom now just drove it all home with me. I just couldn't figure out why.

The rest of the drive was silent.

***

"Your dad took me duck hunting," Chad announced, his hands tight on the steering wheel of the Vanagon as we bounced down the road.

My mouth dropped open and I clutched the armrest. Just moments earlier, I'd been thinking he smelled like sandalwood and coconut oil. Now I wondered if that was to cover the scent of gunpowder. "What? My dad doesn't hunt."

"He does now. I knew you wouldn't approve of me going, but what choice did I have?" His hair was standing on end, like he'd continually been running his hands through it.

"You didn't shoot any of those poor innocent creatures, did you?"

"No, I had the opportunity, but I wouldn't do that. I missed on purpose. I wasn't supposed to be hunting at all, because I didn't have a permit, but your dad put the gun in my hands and insisted I give it a . . . shot."

I narrowed my eyes. "That's horrible."

"Your dad has horrible aim. I guess that's a good thing."

I crossed my arms now, unsettled with the images in my head. "I guess."

Chad's expression cleared. "So, now that that's out in the open, where are we going?"

I glanced down at my lap and searched through a couple of different papers to find Winnie's address. I'd had to search through my parents' files to find the floral information—Sharo seemed to have misplaced her copy.

I'd gone through some old bills from my father's practice, Sharo's bill—she was pricey—and the catering invoice, and finally I'd found the florist. However, the paper I stared at now was one where I'd scribbled an address. "We're headed toward 416 Hawthorne Avenue."

"The florist, right?"

I shook my head, bracing myself for his reaction. "I have one stop to make first."

"So, what's at 416 Hawthorne Avenue?"

"It's the address of the dog walker, Winnie Dubois."

"You figured out her name?"

I shrugged. "I have my ways."

"Are you sure you want to keep pursuing this, Sierra?"

That was a great question. I sighed and glanced out the window. "I guess I feel like Big Boy came to me for help."

"The dog?"

I nodded. He sounded like he'd never been around me before. "Yes, the dog. I realize that sounds weird. But whether I like it or not, I'm involved."

"You could become uninvolved at any time." He cast me a knowing glance.

"I'll just do this and then I'm done," I promised. My throat ached as I said the words.

"What if Big Boy comes back?"

My throat went dry. I didn't want to lie, and the question was legitimate. Chad knew me all too well. "I don't know."

Chad reached over and squeezed my hand. "I think your tenacity is admirable."

Relief washed through me. Why did I always think everyone would react like my parents would? "Really?"

"Of course I do. You're passionate and dedicated, and you fight for what you believe in. What's there not to admire about that?"

"Marrying you was the best thing I ever did." I leaned forward and kissed his cheek.

"You're going to make me blush."

"You've been a real trooper being here, Chad. Thank you." I sincerely meant those words.

"Only for you."

As I let those words wrap around my heart for a moment, I pointed to an approaching street. "Turn here."

Chad did.

A few minutes later we pulled to a stop in front of a little Cape Cod–style house. There was a beat-up-looking sedan parked out front. The mailbox at the street gaped open, an overflowing stack of letters and flyers inside.

The feeling of grief intensified in my gut.

Could I be wrong again? It was entirely possible. I'd

been convinced that the body had been Mrs. Lennox's initially. I was playing detective here, and Chad was right: I really had no good reason to be this involved. It would be just as easy for me to walk away and leave this to the police. But, for some reason, I was hanging on.

"You sure you want to do this?" Chad asked as he put his van in park.

I nodded. "Yes, I'm sure."

Without any more hesitation, I climbed from the car and tepidly walked up the front steps. Before I could second-guess myself, I rapped on the door.

It wasn't a surprise when no one answered.

The sinking feeling in my gut sank even lower. In one way, I had an answer, but in another sense I'd reached a dead end.

"You with the po-lice?" someone called.

I spotted a neighbor standing at the fence. She was meth-addict skinny and had thin hair, bags under her eyes, and dull skin.

I shook my head. "No, I'm not."

"The po-lice were here just an hour ago. Is Winnie okay?"

I shrugged. "I'm not sure. I was looking for a dog walker."

"Winnie's the best. Loves her animals. She didn't have her own because she wasn't home enough, but she took the time to pet any dog that came past her house. Never understood why she didn't drum up business here in the neighborhood, though. Maybe she was too expensive for this area."

"You seen her lately?"

She shook her head. "Not in a few days."

Chad pointed to the car. "Is that hers?"

"No, that's her roommate's, but she's in Europe for the semester, so it's just been sitting there for the past month or two."

I nodded. "Thank you."

"Who did you say you were again?"

"Someone interested in dog walking." With that, I climbed back into the car. We had to pick up the flowers, stop by my mom's office, and get home.

And, as I'd promised Chad, I was done with this, whether I wanted to be or not.

***

On the way home, the rain, which had faded to a drizzle for about thirty minutes, now poured down in buckets.

Things weren't looking good for my parents' celebration, which was scheduled to start in three hours.

When I wasn't feeling bad for my parents, I was also thinking about Big Boy. Where was he right now? I hated to think about him being out in this mess, but there was little I could do to help him.

Just as we pulled onto my parents' street, a loud

boom filled the air. I glanced at Chad. "That can't be good."

By the time we walked into the house, I knew what the noise was. Lightning must have hit nearby, because the power was out.

My mom was semi-panicked, and not even the flowers I carried in my arms cheered her up. She'd been getting dressed for tonight and slipped back to her room. My dad followed, and I let them go.

In case I hadn't mentioned this yet, I'd never been good at cheering my mom up.

Sharo paced on her cell phone, Aunt Yori was watching some kind of anime on her iPad, my sister was playing a board game with her husband, and Greg read a book in the corner.

Just as I sat on the couch beside Chad, my phone buzzed. I didn't recognize the number, but I knew it was local thanks to the area code. The only local person I'd given my number to was Detective Meadows, so it was no surprise when I heard her voice.

"The more I learn, the more guilty you look," she started.

"I'm not guilty."

"You obviously figured out who Winnie Dubois was, and you went to her house today. Try to cover up a clue you left behind?"

"Of course not. I was actually looking for Big Boy."

"The dog." Her voice was dull with disbelief.

"That's correct."

"Why would you do that?"

"It's a nasty day outside. Your department lost him, so someone's got to look out for the dog."

"I'd tread very carefully, Mrs. Davis. Very carefully."

Her words heated my cheeks. She was right. I was dealing with law enforcement right now. I had to be more respectful. "Of course."

"If you know something you're not telling us, we can bring you in for impeding a police investigation. You realize that, right?"

"Now I do."

"I'll be in touch."

No sooner had I hung up than Dr. Moto came into the room. He shook his head solemnly as he took his seat across from us. He sighed, his shoulders slumping. "I just got some bad news."

More bad news? How much more could one group of people receive in a weekend? "What's wrong?" I asked.

"My assistant is dead."

I tilted my head, wondering exactly where this conversation would lead. "I'm sorry to hear that. What happened?"

"No one knows. But apparently, her body was found in the woods yesterday."

CHAPTER 16

"The woman we found in the woods was your assistant?" I tamped down the excitement in my voice.

Chad put his hand on my knee to ground me. I took a deep breath, remembering that I really didn't have a personal stake in this, so I needed to bring my emotions down a notch.

"That's right. She walked dogs on the side. I gave her name and number to a couple of people on this street, as a matter of fact," he said.

"Why would you do that?"

"I live only one street over. The poor girl was struggling to make ends meet, and I always want to reward people for trying to make a go of things on their own. I figured it was the least I could do for her. I do interact quite a bit with the people here thanks to the community meetings."

Why didn't I know any of this? I carefully avoided Chad's gaze, because I knew I'd promised not to get involved. But I wasn't really getting involved right now. I was just asking questions.

"I thought my parents liked it here because there was no homeowners association."

"It's not a homeowners association. It's a civic league. We've had some thefts in the area lately, so we felt it was a good idea to all unite in order to prevent crimes from happening."

"Do the police have any idea what happened to Winnie?"

Dr. Moto shook his head. "Not that I know of. They just called asking me when I'd seen her last."

"When did you see her last?" I asked.

"She came into work on Wednesday. Thursday was her day off because she had classes. Then Friday I had taken off so I could spend time with the family here. I called the office manager, and she confirmed that Winnie never came in yesterday. We had no idea . . ."

"Was she mixed up with the wrong crowd?" I continued, trying not to sound overeager.

He shrugged. "Not that I know of. I did not exactly ask her about her social life, though. There are professional boundaries in place."

"Has she acted out of the ordinary lately?"

He let out a feeble laugh. "Sierra, you ask many questions. I know not the answers."

"Would anyone in your office have the answers?" I didn't know when to leave well enough alone, I supposed.

"Perhaps Shaunda would. Would you like her number?"

"Would it be weird if I said yes?"

He laughed again. "I will call her first and make

sure it is okay."

"One more question." Push, push, push. It was what I did best at times.

"Yes, Sierra?"

Bless his heart—one of my favorite southern expressions—my godfather didn't even look annoyed like anyone in his right mind might be.

"Do you think any of your neighbors are capable of murder?"

"Sierra, anyone is capable of murder. Anyone."

I wanted to ask more questions. I really did. But before I could, movement in the backyard caught my eye.

My heart raced when I realized that Big Boy had returned.

***

My mom reappeared at the base of the stairs, almost like she had a sixth sense that alerted her when something was about to go wrong.

"Someone get that dog!" she shouted.

Chad and I took off. We stepped outside into the rain. Big Boy ran toward me—until he saw that I was running for him. Then he turned on his tail, like he thought we were playing with him, and he dodged us.

I was unsure whether to run or wait, but with an audience peering out the windows at me, I decided to sprint after him.

Bad idea.

He knocked over an entire row of chairs. What he didn't knock over, he splattered mud on.

"You go that way!" I shouted.

Chad and I split up and finally had the dog cornered at the far end of the yard. Chairs bordered one side, a fence on the other, and Chad and I covered the paths of escape.

I decided to talk sweet to him. "Come on, Big Boy. It's okay."

The dog paused and stared at me. He stayed where he was, and I crept close, knowing better than to lunge at him. I treaded very, very carefully, even resisting the urge to wipe the rain out of my eyes.

Just as I thought I'd reached him, he jumped over a row of chairs. Somehow, in the process, he connected with the lights that were dangling from poles above us and jerked them all down. It all happened so fast that I nearly found myself tangled in the wires.

Then, just as quickly as the whole fiasco had begun, Big Boy galloped off.

I turned toward Chad. We were both wet, covered in mud, and wrapped in string lights. Around us, it looked like a hurricane had come through. Chairs were everywhere. The lights were down. A couple of tables had been knocked over.

I looked back at my parents' house and saw them gaping at me from the window. So much for cleaning everything up before they noticed.

***

"The ceremony is canceled!" my mom cried, throwing her hands in the air. She wore her nicely tailored dress, a rose number that accentuated her tiny waist. Her hair was pulled back on the sides with little flowered combs, and her makeup looked perfect.

Meanwhile, I—again—had mud all over me and smelled like nature. I dared not to sit on anything. I barely wanted to come inside, but I'd had no choice but to face the music, so to speak. Chad had been smart and immediately disappeared to the guesthouse to clean up.

I tried to think of some solutions that would make everything better. "We can move the ceremony inside."

"No, it's no use. It's all ruined!"

"Oh, Mai. Don't give up." Sharo handed my mom a tissue.

A fire lit in my mom's eyes. "I'm not giving up. But I am going to give someone a piece of my mind."

My mom stood, the tissue falling to the floor as she stormed toward the door. My initial thought was to stop her. It was immediately followed by the thought that I should join her.

"Mai—" my dad started.

"I've got it, Dad." *Because I've been so good at resolving conflict with my mom in the past.*

I followed her out the door. Just me and Mom. We

said nothing as we strode through the rain.

My mom's hair stuck to her face, her mascara ran down her cheeks, and her clothes clung to her skin. I'd never, ever seen my mom like this.

As we got closer to the Lennoxes', I quickened my steps to catch up with her. "Mom, do you know what you're going to say?"

"I'll figure it out." She looked straight ahead, nearly militant in the way she held herself.

I felt like I should talk some sense into her, but I didn't. My mom was intelligent, educated, and successful. Certainly she had this. She didn't need me giving her advice.

And, for a moment, I saw myself. I'd never, ever seen any part of myself in my parents. But today I did.

Did my mom actually have emotions at one time in her life? Had she had passion? Spontaneity?

I found it hard to comprehend. I needed to sleep on this. The thoughts were almost too much.

As we hurried down the soppy sidewalk, voices drifted out from the Lennoxes' open windows. "I really think this new fur will take us over the top in sales," a woman said.

I cringed. New fur? What were they talking about?

"I agree. Fur collectors everywhere will be in line to get their hands on this," a man said.

The idea of *101 Dalmatians* floated through my mind again. I shook my head. No, they didn't have Big Boy for the sole purpose of breeding him and making fur out of his pups. That was morbid, the stuff that only happened in . . . uh, children's stories?

Without any hesitation, my mom marched up to the Lennoxes' front door and rang the bell. The rain pounded us as we stood there, with no stoop to cover our heads. I was sure we were a sight to behold.

The door opened and Mrs. Lennox appeared. Her face went from annoyed to surprised when she spotted us. "What in the world . . . ?"

"Your dog has ruined my recommitment ceremony. It's ruined! And it's all that dog's fault!"

"What?" Mrs. Lennox pulled her black sweater tighter across her shoulders.

I couldn't blame her. The accusation might throw anyone off, especially coming from my mother.

"That dog of yours! He just tromped all over my backyard. The ceremony has been canceled. Are you happy now?"

"Mai, would you like to come inside?" Mrs. Lennox asked. "Maybe out of the rain for a moment?"

My mom did just that, and I followed suit. Instantly, I remembered finding the blood here. I remembered sneaking into the house with Chad.

Was I in the house of a killer?

"Now, if you'd slow down, maybe we can talk things over," Mrs. Lennox started.

Reggie, wearing a headset phone and holding a yellow legal pad, joined us as we stood in a circle in the grand foyer. He didn't appear to be as annoyed today.

Had I caught him on a bad day before?

My mom poured out the whole story, and to my surprise, the Lennoxes listened to everything. And I did mean *everything*.

Mother ended with "My first ceremony was ruined by a dog, too. My roommate had an Akita. He jumped on me the morning of the wedding and left a horrible scratch across my cheek. All the makeup in the world wouldn't cover it up. There was nothing perfect about that day. I wanted this one to be different. I wanted to make things right."

The ice around my heart cracked a little.

"I'm so sorry," Mrs. Lennox finally said. She slipped an arm around my mother. "Let me get you some hot tea before you get sick."

She led her off into the kitchen.

And I stood there with Reggie.

Favor was on my side.

He stared at me before finally saying, "Sorry about the ceremony."

I nodded. "It happens."

"Do you happen to know where my dog went?"

He actually sounded like he cared, I mused. Interesting. Was that because he wanted the dog's fur?

"He scampered off into the woods."

He grunted. "I have filed a complaint about the police department for losing him in the first place."

"I thought you didn't even like him."

"Whatever gave you that impression?" He looked at

me like I'd grown a tail and two floppy ears.

"You didn't even notice him that day after your supposed nosebleed. You left him outside with strangers."

He sighed and rubbed his mustache. "I'd just come home to a house surrounded by police cars. I was slightly distracted, and later I felt terrible about it."

I was going to go for it and put one of my theories out there. "Rumor has it that you hired a dog walker because you despised having to take care of the dog yourself."

"What? Who told you that?" His voice climbed in pitch.

I shrugged. "I have my sources."

"Mrs. Jericho," he growled. "I hired a dog walker because the girl looked like she needed a hand, you know what I mean? Plus, I like Dr. Moto."

"What about the argument you got into with her?"

He dropped his yellow pad onto a nearby table and used his hands like a preacher might to drive home a point in his sermon. "It was because of her boyfriend. I didn't mind her coming. But she brought her boyfriend with her. He looked unsavory, if you know what I mean. I didn't approve, and I told her in no uncertain terms that if she brought him again, she was done."

Interesting. "How did she respond to that?"

"Her face went white and she nodded, saying it wouldn't happen again. Of course, that was the last time I saw her. I have to say Horace really liked her."

"Horace?"

"My dog." Now he really stared at me like I was crazy.

"Oh." He'd become Big Boy in my mind, and I couldn't imagine him as a Horace.

My mom came back into the room with Mrs. Lennox, and she looked considerably calmer now. I was considering the possibility that she'd been poisoned, or some other nefarious reason for her change in behavior.

That's when I noticed a speckle of blood on the floor.

It was fresh.

I looked up just as Reggie reached for his nose.

Sure enough, he had a nosebleed.

He'd been telling the truth after all.

CHAPTER 17

After her talk with Mrs. Lennox, my mom decided the ceremony would go on. A Catholic church down the street had been reserved as a backup, and all the details were being worked out by Reina and Sharo at the moment.

Sharo hung up the phone and turned to address the rest of us as we stood in the living room, each afraid in our own way of saying anything that would set my mom off. At least, that was the vibe I got.

Sharo frowned, and I braced myself for whatever she was about to say. It wasn't going to be good. "Mr. and Mrs. Nakamura, can I speak with you?"

"Just go ahead and say whatever it is. We're all in this together," my mom said.

She rubbed her hands nervously. "I'm afraid there was a misunderstanding. The church is being used tonight for another wedding."

"What? I thought you reserved it!" My mom's nostrils flared.

Sharo looked away nervously. "I actually thought that you had reserved it. Isn't the priest's wife your patient?"

"Priests are celibate!" Veins bulged at my mom's neck. "You were supposed to be on top of this. I thought you were the best?"

Sharo stepped closer, her gaze apologetic. "I know. I'm so very sorry. They said we could use the church tomorrow evening after mass."

"This is a sign. None of this was supposed to happen. I don't know what I was thinking." With that, my mom stormed off.

My dad followed after her.

The rest of us stood there, a sea of awkwardness between us. Finally, my sister cleared her throat. "I need to make some phone calls. Would anyone like to help?"

Sharo, Greg, and Aunt Yori volunteered. Meanwhile, I volunteered to take some food out for people to eat. At least it was something to keep me occupied. I disappeared into my thoughts for a moment as I pulled out bread and condiments.

Something just seemed a little different about my parents, and I wasn't sure what. This whole ceremony seemed strange and unlike something they'd want to do. My mom was much more emotional than I was used to. I knew things changed with time, but it was hard for me to think about my parents changing also.

Chad shimmied up beside me. "You okay?"

I nodded. "I am. I'm just thinking about how strange it is to come home."

"I think we all experience that to some degree,

Sierra."

I turned as I heard someone coming down the stairs. My dad stood there, and he was looking at me. There was a look in his eyes that I couldn't quite identify.

"Is Mom okay?"

He nodded curtly. "She'll be fine. She's resting at the moment. May I have a moment, Sierra?"

Great. What had I done now? I didn't ask that, but instead I nodded. "Sure."

"You come, too." He pointed to Chad.

This really wasn't good. Had he found out I was married? Did he blame me for this whole ceremony being ruined? A feeling of impending doom continued to grow inside me.

We followed him upstairs to a room located above the garage. I hadn't come in here in years. Last I knew, it was an office.

But when my dad opened the door now, I sucked in a deep breath. Lights — like those that might be found on a fashion week runway — lined the edges of the room. The walls were painted a deep blue with silver stars randomly placed. Even the carpet was new, red, and lush.

But the most striking aspect of the room was the mannequins that stood like a horror-movie-inspired army against one wall. One wore a gaudy sequined gown. Another wore a postman outfit. One wore nothing except a cowboy hat. Little spotlights coming from the ceiling highlighted each.

"What?" I whispered.

My dad smiled. "Your mother and I have taken up a new hobby."

I stepped inside and walked on autopilot toward one of the outfits. It was a leather number with a plunging neckline and a naughty-looking slit going up the front.

"What is this?" I felt like I'd stepped into *The Twilight Zone*.

My dad grinned again, looking almost like a little boy. "Your mother and I have taken up a new hobby. We're collecting iconic outfits worn by famous celebrities."

"Are you serious?" I certainly hadn't heard him correctly. Next he would tell me that it was okay to run with scissors.

He nodded and walked toward the leather gown. "It's true. This one was worn by Dolly Parton. It went for more than ten thousand at auction."

"You paid ten thousand for this dress?" My mouth sagged open. Didn't he know how much good that money could do in this world? It could help feed and clothe the homeless!

"I really wanted your mother to have something to look forward to. She was talking about how our wedding was ruined by that Akita, and that's when I suggested renewing our vows. I knew she loved Princess Di, and I found a handkerchief from the royal wedding at an auction. Don't worry—all the proceeds went to a children's charity. Anyway, after we won the handkerchief, we found bidding to be quite addicting. We haven't been able to stop."

"Mother is not this irrational." I stiffened, certain I was being tricked here.

My father's smile slipped, and what almost looked like a touch of sadness swept over his gaze. "It's a new hobby. Life is different now, Sierra, and we are looking for things to do together. We discovered auctions and playing bridge fit both of us well."

"Mom plays bridge?"

Dad nodded. "I do also. Every Wednesday night, like clockwork."

I had to recalculate my thoughts here before I said something disrespectful. "Where did you say you got these outfits?"

"At auction. We usually go into the Big Apple about once a month. It's something fun to do, and we can always get a good return on our investment later."

"These are considered investments?" Chad sounded just as surprised as I felt.

My dad nodded. "Yes. Take this Elvis outfit from his 1958 movie where he played a postman. They're remaking the movie now, so it's expected this clothing may even double in value when the movie is released."

"Elvis, huh?"

He nodded and moved on to the black leather dress. "Marilyn Monroe wore the sequined gown and even signed it."

"Very interesting," I muttered. What else could I say?

My dad turned toward us, the same unreadable expression in his eyes. "This isn't the real reason I asked for you to come up here. There's something I need to tell you, Sierra. The real reason I called you up here is because—"

Before he could finish his sentence, a commotion sounded downstairs.

We all looked at each other and rushed toward the sound.

What had happened now?

***

"Aunt Yori is gone!" my sister whispered to me as everyone gathered in the kitchen. Dr. Moto took over the crisis intervention and stood in the center of the circle sending out search parties.

"What do you mean, gone?" I asked, keeping one ear on Dr. Moto as he directed people to double-check various parts of the house.

"She was here an hour ago, and now no one can find her."

"Did anyone consider maybe she went upstairs to lie down? Or, as crazy as this may sound, maybe she just went to the bathroom?"

My sister rolled her eyes. "Of course we did. We checked those places, and she's not there. We're checking again. If you haven't been able to tell, she has a bit of a drinking problem. Mom is afraid she'll wander off and get herself in trouble."

"Wander off?"

"Like into the woods behind the house."

That made sense. The last thing we needed was another disaster this weekend. My sister was right: we had to find Aunt Yori now.

"Chad and I can go outside," I spoke up. "We'll search the backyard and the guesthouse."

"Thank you," Dr. Moto said. "Who wants to cover the street?"

Chad and I hurried outside into the dreary, getting-colder-by-the-hour day. At the edge of the deck, I yelled for my aunt. As I expected, there was no response.

We'd check the backyard and the guesthouse. If we didn't find her, we'd search the woods behind the property. I hoped it didn't come to that, because if my aunt was lost in the woods, there was a greater chance of her getting hurt.

As we walked around the perimeter of the backyard, I whispered, "I think my parents are going crazy. They're losing their minds, Chad. What else would explain that celebrity memorabilia upstairs?"

"People can change, Sierra."

"Not my parents!" He didn't know them like I did. They were seriously losing their minds or something. That was the only explanation I could think of.

"I think it's kind of funny. You're right; they don't seem like the type to be starstruck about celebrities."

I peered behind a bush. "And another thought. What do you think about *101 Dalmatians*?"

"I really liked the part where the dogs started eating spaghetti and ended up kissing—"

"No, that's *Lady and the Tramp*."

"That's right." He nodded as everything appeared to come back to him. "*101* is the one with all the puppies, and the mean lady is trying to capture them."

"Right. What do you think about it playing out in real life?"

"What?" He searched behind some shrubs.

I considered not telling him my theory. But I'd come this far. As crazy as it might sound, I needed to just spill everything. "I wonder if the Lennoxes are planning on making fur out of Big Boy."

His expression made it clear that Aunt Yori and I were definitely related. Maybe we both had the crazy gene. "They certainly wouldn't have let the dog slip away that easily and without that much concern if he was going to become a coat."

I peered behind the shed where many of the larger pool supplies were stored. "He could just be the stud. Maybe they're already done with him, so they don't care anymore."

"You really think someone's trying to make clothing out of dogs?"

"I know it sounds crazy, but I overheard the

Lennoxes talking about a new fur they're going to introduce. Then I thought about Big Boy and how pretty his coat is."

Chad slowly swung his head back and forth, almost as if he was trying to figure out how to break bad news to me. "They'd be taking it pretty far if they did that, Sierra. Aren't there laws against that? Certainly animal cruelty, if nothing else."

I pulled my glasses off, wiping the droplets of rain from the lenses. "I don't know. People do crazy things. Kill elephants for their tusks. Murder tigers and drink their blood thinking they'll live longer. There's no end to what people might do to further advance their own agendas."

"History can't dispute that."

"Maybe the dog walker discovered their scheme, and they killed her for it. That would be motive for murder."

"I wouldn't get too hung up on that theory. It's pretty out there. Right now, we should just concentrate on finding your aunt."

I nodded. "You're right. Let's keep looking."

Aunt Yori was nowhere in the backyard. But I noticed the door to the guesthouse was cracked open. Chad and I exchanged that married-couple look, the one where we didn't have to say a word to know what the other was thinking.

With a nod, we approached the door, ready to find out what was going on inside.

CHAPTER 18

Chad stepped inside first. He glanced around and then motioned me to follow. He put a finger over his lips to signal to stay quiet.

The guesthouse appeared to be undisturbed. Still, we moved with amazing stealth across the tile floor.

The kitchen and living room were clear. Chad started toward the bedroom. He threw the door open, scanned the interior, and then shrugged. I followed him inside, calculating each move.

The last thing I needed was for a killer to be hanging out here and for us to stumble into his lair. I had too much on the line to be killed by a psycho.

Alas, the bedroom was empty, though.

"Where else can we check?" I asked.

"There are a couple of closets. I guess we should look inside to make sure no one's hiding there. After that, we check the woods."

Chad pulled the first closet door open, and all it revealed were pool supplies—chemicals and filters and cleaning nets. No one in there.

As we approached the closet in the living room, I thought I heard a thump. My nerves tightened at the sound.

A killer wouldn't be thumping, right? Unless he wanted to lure us to the closet.

I grabbed a poker beside the fireplace. Chad silently counted to three and then jerked the door open.

Sure enough, there was Aunt Yori! A cloth had been shoved into her mouth, but her hands and feet weren't bound. She blinked when she saw us, a certain haziness in her gaze.

Chad quickly helped me pull her out. She still smelled like alcohol.

I pulled her gag out. Her eyes were glazed as she opened and shut her mouth, lapping a dry-sounding tongue against the top of her mouth. "Am I sleepwalking?"

"What happened?" I asked. I held onto her elbow while she found her balance.

"I don't know. One minute I was raiding the mini-bar in here. Then someone put a bag over my head. Next thing I knew, I was in here. I thought I was being swept away to a surprise bachelorette party. I guess not."

Surprise bachelorette party? "Do you remember anything about this person?"

She shook her head. "Not a thing. Except she muttered something about stitching."

"Stitching?"

"Maybe it was snitching. Yes, that was it. Snitching. So then I thought it was some kind of new bachelorette party game."

"You said *she*?" I clarified.

"That's right. It was a woman. Or a man with a high-pitched voice. Pretty sure that wasn't the case."

A woman. That still left either Mrs. Lennox or Mrs. Jericho. Either could have easily slipped into the backyard and done the deed.

"I felt like I was in Vegas for a minute." She sighed. "I just love Vegas."

I glanced at Chad. My crazy aunt Yori was just as crazy as ever. What in the world was she talking about? Had something nefarious happened? Or had my aunt wandered into this closet of her own accord?

Maybe this mystery was hitting closer to home than I thought.

***

That night, after my aunt Yori was deemed okay by both my mother and father, everyone attempted to act normal. However, there was an undercurrent of anxiety that trickled through the room. Everyone was on edge now, wondering just what was going on.

My mom wanted to call the police, but Aunt Yori had insisted that whoever had put her in the closet had just been joking. Then she started talking crazy again, mentioning Las Vegas and meeting celebrities. My mom and dad had looked at each other, and I could read their thoughts: they thought Aunt Yori was losing it and had been drinking too much. I was inclined to agree.

With the power back on and Aunt Yori tucked into bed, most of the guests who weren't staying at the house had left. Dr. Moto's nurse called me.

I slipped away from the crowd. They'd just begun a rousing game of Scrabble. I was happy to say that when I left, Chad was ahead of everyone else thanks to one word: *zoologist*.

"The doctor said you wanted to talk to me," she started.

I sat in the stairway, just like I used to do when I was younger, when I waited for my parents to come home at night. I hadn't thought about that in a long time, and the memory felt a bit like a slap to my heart.

"I have some questions about Winnie Dubois. I was hoping you could answer them," I started.

"I can try."

"Have you talked to her since Wednesday?"

"No, ma'am. She said she was going home after work and wanted to rest. She was tired from working two jobs and going to school."

"Why did she work two jobs?"

"Same reason most people do: she was strapped for cash. She had bills to pay, including student loans. You do what you have to do."

"I heard she was dating someone."

"Yeah. His name was Nick, I think. He only came into the office once."

"What did you think about him?"

She made an uncertain grunt. "I don't know. He looked a little rough. You know how it is. You try not to judge a book by its cover, but sometimes it's hard."

"Did they have any problems?"

"If they did, she didn't talk to me about them."

Well, this conversation wasn't getting me anywhere. Not really.

"I guess Dr. Moto liked her if he recommended her services throughout the neighborhood. That spoke volumes about her character."

"Well, between you and me, I smell something fishy."

Now we were getting somewhere!

"What?"

"The doctor signed off on a form. He was in a hurry that day. Anyway, he didn't read closely enough, and he shouldn't have given an okay in this particular case for this particular medicine. Winnie caught it and showed it to him. He was so grateful that he said anytime she needed something, he owed her one. That's when she mentioned the dog-walking business."

"Is that fishy?" I asked.

"The fishy part is that I think she forged his signature on that paper."

"Why would you think that?"

"I walked in and saw her doing something with that stack of papers. When she saw me, she got all flustered and muttered that I should knock before walking into a room."

"So you think she set the doctor up, hoping to be in his good graces?"

"Yeah, that's exactly what I think."

CHAPTER 19

So maybe Winnie wasn't as innocent as I thought.

Maybe some other people weren't as innocent as I thought, either. Like the doctor. But my godfather didn't seem like the type to be manipulated.

What if Winnie's manipulation went further than just getting dog-sitting jobs? What if there was something far greater at stake? Something worth murdering over?

However, my aunt Yori thought the person who'd pushed her into the closet was a woman. Dr. Moto did have a higher-pitched voice, but certainly my aunt would have recognized him.

I shook my head, trying to make sense of things. Tomorrow evening, Chad and I were leaving. If I didn't have the answers by then, I probably would never have them. And that seemed like a shame, kind of like an unfinished book or movie. These things needed resolution.

A scratch sounded at the window. I tensed. Until I looked over.

Big Boy was there, his paws splayed against the glass and his tongue hanging out.

He was back! Again!

Before anyone else saw me — namely, my mother — I slipped outside. The rain had stopped, but the ground was still sopping wet. Why had he come back? He seemed to appear at the worst times.

Someone stepped outside right behind me. "Sierra! What are you doing?"

It was Chad.

As I started to answer, Big Boy bounded over and gave me a muddy doggy kiss.

"Should have guessed," Chad mumbled.

"You caused a lot of trouble earlier," I told him.

He barked at me.

"Shh," I insisted, looking back at the house. The last thing I needed was to stir the pot any more.

With that admonition, the dog turned and ran toward the back fence.

I had the distinct feeling he was trying to tell me something. I took off after him.

This definitely hadn't been a boring trip home. Anything but.

Suddenly, Big Boy put on his brakes. So did I, for that matter.

I scrunched my nose as Big Boy started to do his business by the gate. I felt like I was invading his privacy as I stood there and stared at him.

Chad caught up with me and moaned. "Disgusting."

"It happens."

When Big Boy was done, he bounded over the fence and disappeared out of sight. I almost went after him, but I decided Big Boy might do better on his own than he would with me.

Besides, he'd just left us another present.

I turned to Chad. "Can you subtly go get a plastic bag? There are some gloves in the upstairs bathroom. Maybe get some of those, too. They're in between the surgical masks and gauze."

"Okay." He took a step and stopped. "Are you going to . . . ?"

"I'm just going to protect the feces in case it rains again." I pulled out my cell. "I'm also calling the detective."

"You promise?"

"Of course!"

As he hurried toward the house, I made good on my assurance. Detective Meadows said she was on her way.

Since I was waiting, I bent down closer to inspect the scat in front of me. This was not my favorite way to investigate, not in any terms. But I knew the police thought there could be evidence in the waste Big Boy had left behind.

They were right.

There, woven in the pile, was a gold chain.

I looked left and right to make sure no one was around, and then I squatted down. I grabbed a stick and nudged the pile of manure. In the middle was a charm.

I pulled out my cell phone and took a picture.

I couldn't quite make out the design, only that it had several circles around each other, almost like a treble clef. I couldn't be sure, and to investigate further would mean digging in more . . . literally.

Tampering with evidence would be a little too obvious.

Just then, on the other side of the fence, I heard a twig break.

My skin tightened.

What was that?

It wasn't Big Boy. Everything about that dog was big, and he didn't know how to be quiet.

No, I had a feeling that was a person.

Did he or she know I was here? Were they waiting to pounce on me?

That was my best guess.

I also remembered seeing Mrs. Jericho peering over the side of this fence. Maybe that was her *modus operandi*. Maybe she came and went from my parents' property by crossing backyards until she reached this gate.

I could hardly breathe. I didn't dare stand.

What if the intruder was watching me? What if he or she had a gun trained on me from above? What if I was basically a sitting duck right now?

"I got the bag!" Chad shouted, bursting from the house.

The sudden outburst was enough to startle me. Totally startle me.

Startle me enough that I lost my balance, and my hand landed right in . . . Big Boy's present.

CHAPTER 20

"You're telling me the evidence has been compromised?" Detective Meadows said as we stood in the backyard, both darkness and dampness surrounding us. Everyone else had been directed to stay inside.

I nodded, hating the stench that covered my hand. "That's correct. It was an accident. I was trying to protect the, uh . . . manure . . . when I was startled. Unfortunately, my hand landed right in the pile."

I couldn't be sure, but she may have stifled a smile.

The CSI techs, however, weren't amused. They swabbed my hands, just in case there was any trace evidence there.

Just before they bagged the rest of the doodie, I glanced down. It was hard to see, but I could make out just a little more of the design of the necklace than I did before. Definitely a ring of circles with a line in the middle. I hadn't seen the design before.

Thunder cracked overhead. Another storm was coming.

I really wanted to get inside and take a shower. There was one other thing I needed to mention first.

"By the way, Detective Meadows, have you looked into Winnie's boyfriend? I think his name is Nick."

She paused, a very serious look in her eyes. "I have been investigating, Mrs. Davis. That's what I'm paid to do."

I understood her implications. She didn't appreciate me questioning her or snooping. I got that. "I'm not trying to overstep my boundaries."

She took a step away but hesitated before turning back to me. "If you must know, he's dead."

"Dead?" Surprise saturated my voice. I had not expected that. "How?"

I didn't really expect her to answer. I wasn't sure how much information was public versus private. But the words slipped from my lips.

"He was electrocuted, if you must know. While trying to steal copper wiring from an AC unit the next neighborhood over."

"That's horrible."

The detective nodded. "It will be in tomorrow's paper, so I figured it couldn't hurt to tell you now, especially since every time I turn around, you seem to be in the thick of things."

"That dog just likes me."

She stared at my poopy hand. "Obviously."

I deserved that.

The police finished up and promised to be in touch. All I could think was: Winnie's boyfriend was dead. How did that tie in? Had Winnie gotten the job as a dog walker just to learn the schedules of residents in the neighborhood? I knew there was big money in selling copper. Was she that desperate for some extra cash?

And could it be a coincidence that her boyfriend had died nearly around the same time Winnie had, at least according to my estimations?

As soon as the police walked way, I wiped my hand using a wet paper towel Chad held out to me. I couldn't wait to go wash up properly. But there was one other thing I had to do first.

"You can come out now, Mrs. Jericho," I called over the fence.

Silence.

Chad stared at me a moment like I was crazy. I couldn't blame him.

"I know you're there," I repeated. "I'm pretty sure I can run faster than you, so all I have to do is open that gate and I'll catch you."

At once I had a vision of Tommy Mitford chasing me on the school playground in third grade with a booger on the end of his finger. Was this how juvenile I'd become? I let out a mental sigh.

Just as I reached for the gate latch, a head bobbed up. Mrs. Jericho frowned and crossed her arms. "How'd you know I was back there?"

"I heard a stick crack."

"How'd you know it was me?" Her voice rose, already high pitched but climbing into the stratosphere with every word.

People's voices were doing that a lot lately.

"Because you're the typical nosy neighbor, for one. Secondly, this seems to be the way you like to come to my family's yard. And finally, who better to spy on what's going on than the murderer herself?"

She gasped. "I'm not a murderer."

"How'd you get that dent in the hood of your car?" I hadn't been able to stop thinking about it all day. And the fact that she'd had it detailed shortly after. Maybe to remove the blood?

"What dent?"

"Don't play dumb. I saw it." Thunder clapped overhead again.

She frowned. "I hit a deer. There. Are you happy?"

"When?"

"A few days ago."

"Is that why you had your car detailed?"

She gasped again. "Have you been digging into my background? Uncovering how I've spent the past several days? Researching who I am?"

"In a sense." I shrugged. I really hadn't gone that far, and it was a fluke I'd learned about her car being detailed. She didn't have to know that, though.

She raised her chin. "I suppose you know, then, that I lost my job with Morrison's Music two months ago."

I had no idea. But I'd pretend like I did. "Motive. That's what I call that!"

"No!" she exclaimed. "That's why I had my yard sale. I needed some extra cash. I like earning things the old-fashioned way—with hard work and sweat."

I wondered if hard work and sweat might include stealing copper wires. Was she working with Winnie and Nick for this whole scheme? Had something gone horribly wrong? Greed, betrayal, envy . . . there were so many possibilities.

"What did you do at Morrison's again?" I asked, hoping she wouldn't see through me.

"I was in sales. Why?"

For a music company? Could that have been some kind of music note on the end of the necklace? I wasn't a musician, so I hadn't recognized it.

"I'm sure being fired for . . . the reasons you were . . . had to be upsetting." I was fishing; I admitted it. But I wanted more information.

"Budget cuts have hit us all. What can I say? I just never expected to be a fatality." Tears glistened in her eyes. "I'd been loyal to the company for ten years, you know. It's all I had. No family, no kids, only my cat."

What if Mrs. Jericho discovered what Winnie was doing—maybe she even wanted in on it?—and the two had a fight? What if Mrs. Jericho, in a moment of rage, ran over Winnie?

Motive, means, and opportunity were coming together in my mind.

"Whatever happened to that deer you hit, Mrs. Jericho?"

Her face went pale. "I left it in the road."

"Where?"

"Just a few streets over."

"When?"

She gulped. "Wednesday night."

The approximate night Winnie had died.

"I'm going to have to call the police, Mrs. Jericho. I think you killed Winnie. Ran her over. She probably limped off into the woods for help. Either that, or you drug her there. Either way, you're a cold-blooded killer."

I expected her to deny it. To become defiant.

Instead, she burst into tears.

"You're right! I did it! It's all my fault!"

CHAPTER 21

It didn't take long for Detective Meadows to arrive again. By that time, a small crowd had gathered in the backyard. It still thundered overhead, and every once in a while, the sky would spit out a few chilly droplets. The floodlights helped illuminate the environment some.

Mrs. Jericho was telling her story to Detective Meadows.

"I was driving home at night. It was dark. Really dark. The lights had gone out in the neighborhood that night. I admit—I was upset and crying because I'd lost my job and nothing seemed to be going right. That's when, out of nowhere, this woman appeared in the middle of the street. She'd run from the woods. She stopped right there. I slammed on the brakes, but I couldn't miss her. I crashed into her and panicked. I didn't know what to do."

"What next?" Detective Meadows asked.

"Then I realized it was Winnie. I got my sense back and got out of the car. I went to help her, but she pulled herself up from the ground and ran into the woods. I figured she was okay. Then I heard about the dead body, and I knew. I knew!" She wailed again.

"I bet anything that Winnie's boyfriend put her up to this new dog-walking business. He probably wanted her to stake out the neighborhood and figure out when people came and went. It makes perfect sense," I said.

"Mrs. Jericho, you have the right to remain silent . . ." An officer handcuffed her and led her to a squad car.

That's when the detective turned to me. "I feel like I should say good work, but I just can't bring myself to let the words leave my mouth."

I shrugged. "It sounds like a true accident. If she's telling the truth." And I had a feeling Mrs. Jericho was.

Which made me feel sorry for her. Here I'd had this big story worked up in my head about how someone had murdered Winnie because of a nefarious fur scheme or something. All along, it was just bad luck. Being in the wrong place at the wrong time. Making a bad judgment call.

One more thought struck me. "Mrs. Jericho!" I called.

She turned toward me, halfway into the police car. The officer paused also, probably wondering why I was brazen enough to stop him in the middle of an arrest.

"How did the dog get your necklace?" I asked.

"What necklace?"

My muscles tensed.

We were missing something here. I just had no idea what.

***

Everyone else turned in for the night, but I was still wound up. I snuck downstairs, wanting—make that craving—something to eat.

As soon as I opened the refrigerator door, I heard someone behind me. I instantly tensed, expecting the worst.

"Sierra?"

I swirled. It was Greg. Just Greg.

I closed the door and let out a weak laugh. "What are you doing up? You scared me to death."

"I wanted to talk to you, actually. I've been looking for the opportunity to get you alone all weekend."

I took a step back, anticipating where this might be going. Nowhere good. "Oh, really?"

"Sierra . . . as I started to say at rehearsal, I have everything I want in life. Everything except you. I explained that to your parents, and they invited me to come here this weekend."

Oh no! Not this conversation.

"Greg, we both agreed that we weren't right for each other."

"That was then," he said. "Things have changed now."

"They have changed," I agreed. "Greg, Chad—"

"Forget about him."

I cringed. "I can't do that."

"It's not like you're married."

"Well, actually —"

He stepped closer. "We belong together, Sierra."

"About Chad —"

"We're such a better fit." He reached for my arm, and I feared what he might do next.

"Greg, I'm married!"

He dropped his hand and stepped way back like he'd touched fire. "What?"

I nodded, my heart twisted in knots. "It's true. I've been waiting for the right opportunity to tell everyone. I didn't want to ruin my parents' big day."

"I see," he said, suddenly stiff and cold.

"Please don't tell anyone. I'm still trying to figure out how to break the news."

His fierce expression finally softened. "I won't, Sierra. Chad is a lucky man."

"Thank you, Greg."

"I should go." He pointed behind him and crept toward the door.

My heart felt heavy as I watched him go — not because I wanted to be with him, but because I really knew how to mess up situations.

My stomach grumbled. I was still hungry. Some cookies on the breakfast bar beckoned me. I inched closer and picked up one. I brought it to my nose and inhaled the sweet scent.

My mouth salivated. I was so hungry, and this cookie looked so yummy and filling. Just one bite wouldn't hurt anything. I raised it to my lips.

"What are you doing?"

I jumped so high that the cookie flew from my hand and landed in the fishbowl.

Chad stood there, a look unlike any I'd ever seen before in his gaze.

"You scared me." People were doing that a lot lately.

"You were about to eat that cookie."

"I didn't eat it. I only thought about it."

"It was made with eggs," he reminded me.

"You don't know that for sure."

"I do, actually. I saw Ms. Blankenship making them."

I shrugged. "You're sure? Because people are doing some pretty innovative things nowadays, not just vegans."

"Sierra, in the years since I've known you, you've never, ever considered eating meat or any kind of animal byproduct. Yet you almost just ate a cookie. What's going on?"

I shrugged again. "I guess it's just the stress of everything going on lately. It almost got the best of me."

What had just happened? If Chad hadn't just walked in, I would have eaten that cookie. Not only that, but I was concocting real-life *101 Dalmatians* stories, obsessing about a murder that was accidental, and theorizing that my parents had lost their minds. I just didn't feel like myself at all.

He gripped my elbow. "I think you need to get some rest, Sierra, before you do something you regret."

I nodded. "You're right. It's been a busy weekend. I'm not thinking clearly."

"I'll rescue the fish from certain cookie death." He kissed me and started toward the goldfish bowl.

As I shuffled off to bed, all I could think about was that cookie, though.

***

"Sierra, would you get that box you picked up at the office yesterday? Your mom said it's in the garage," Ms. Blankenship asked me in the morning. "The napkins she ordered for the reception are in there, and your mom said we might as well use them for breakfast. No need for everything to go to waste."

I was helping her put together breakfast and had agreed to make the oatmeal, put together a fruit salad, and arrange some pastries. Meanwhile, Ms. Blankenship fixed the sausage and eggs.

I told her okay, went to the garage, and ruffled through things until I found the square little box I'd picked up from my mom's office yesterday. I carried it inside and placed it on the kitchen counter.

"It's good to have you home again, Sierra," Ms. Blankenship said, stirring some scrambled eggs.

"Thanks, Ms. B."

"I know things may seem strange, but I know your

family is glad to have you here, too."

"I'm not so sure about that."

"Life changes all of us, my girl. Sometimes for the better and sometimes for the worse. Your parents aren't who they used to be, even if you might view them as such."

She might as well have been speaking Yoda-ese, because she was making no sense.

Even stranger was the fact that the eggs she cooked actually looked good. I hadn't craved eggs in years. Years. But right now they smelled so good. What was wrong with me?

"Tell me about that boy you brought with you," Ms. B. continued.

"Chad? He's great. He likes me . . . well, for me." I arranged a few pastries on the plate.

"He seems really taken with you. I can tell you have a great bond."

I smiled, one of the first real smiles I'd had since I came home. "Thanks, Ms. B. I appreciate that."

"I always knew you were going to take life by the horns one day. It seems like you've done just that. You've become your own person."

"I've tried to. You were a big part of that, Ms. B. I always felt like you were one of the only people who understood me growing up. You actually cared about what I liked. You listened to me when I spoke. Thank you."

She paused from cooking and gave me a big hug. I

melted into her arms, feeling like a little girl again. "I always wished things were different. I wish that back then, your parents were more like they are now."

"Now?" I blurted the question. Instead of apologizing and claiming I didn't mean it when I did, I shook my head. "Zebras don't change their stripes, Ms. B."

"No, but sometimes things change beneath the surface. You may not see it with your eyes, but you can feel it with your heart."

There she went again with her Yoda-isms. I didn't know what to say. Instead, I found some scissors and sliced the tape on top of the box.

Just then, my mom breezed into the room. "The napkins?" she said. "Great. Just put them on the edge of the table."

I nodded and reached into the box. Instead of pulling out a handful of napkins, I pulled out a handful of . . . pregnancy tests.

"What are you doing?" my mom asked, her voice just below a screech.

I stared at my hand. "What are these?"

"You picked up the wrong box! You were supposed to pick up the napkins!"

"You said the square box. How was I to know?"

My mom waved her hands. "Put those down before someone sees them. That box was supposed to be delivered to the Obstetrics and Gynecology office next door. I set them out so we could take them to their rightful owner."

I resisted a sigh.

Ms. B. was wrong. Some people never changed.

CHAPTER 22

I went to mass with my family after breakfast. It had been my sister's husband's idea, and no one seemed to have any good excuses not to. My mom was still in a foul mood, but she'd gone along with everyone else.

I went to a nondenominational church with my friend Gabby back at home on occasion, and I'd found myself becoming more and more curious about the things the pastor talked about. Gabby and I had some good conversations about religion versus living for Jesus. I wasn't totally sold on the idea of becoming a Christian, but I felt myself inching closer to making a decision.

I couldn't help but think the church back home in Norfolk fit my personality better than the very formal service we were in now. The very formal and proper service, however, fit my parents to a T.

Beside me, my mom was even more solemn than usual. I still couldn't reconcile the idea of my tiger mom deciding to buy clothing worn by celebrities. That fit together about as well as a jackalope.

With Chad on one side of me, I glanced down my row. Reina sat beside me, followed by Mark, Mom,

Dad, Aunt Yori, Greg, and Dr. Moto. The sanctuary was filled, if I had to guess, with around four hundred people, all properly dressed. Everyone rose and sat with the precision of a high school marching band.

I tried to focus on what the priest was saying, but my mind replayed everything that had happened since I arrived here in Connecticut. I'd reviewed everything last night as I lay in bed, as well.

Had Winnie's boyfriend been stealing copper when he forgot to cut the power line? Not only had the power in the entire neighborhood been cut, but he'd also been fried. Maybe Winnie had been with him and freaked out afterward. She darted from the scene.

Since the power was out, the streets were dark. Mrs. Jericho, who'd admittedly been upset, didn't see Winnie sprint into the middle of the road. She'd hit her and come to her senses, but by the time she got out to help, Winnie had fled.

Mrs. Jericho panicked, cleaned her car up, and hoped all would turn out well. But then Winnie's body was discovered in the woods. Guilt had eaten her up, but that guilt quickly turned into fear. She'd tried to make sure no one found out what happened. I was sure the reaction wasn't all that uncommon. She'd probably even made it a point to talk kindly about Winnie that day at the salon in an effort to further cover her tracks.

What didn't fit in my mind was Big Boy's role in all of this. The dog seemed fond of Winnie, that much was obvious. He'd followed her scent into the woods after she died, discovered her body, and led authorities to her.

But what about the necklace? Was it a fluke? Or did it somehow tie in with this case?

"That priest is handsome, Sierra," Aunt Yori blurted, a little too loudly.

Several people turned to stare.

"Want me to see if he's single?"

"Yori!" my mother reprimanded.

I stifled a giggle. Though it had been totally inappropriate—not to mention the fact that I was married now—Aunt Yori always had a way of both breaking and causing tension at the same time.

As the congregation rose for another reading, I glanced around. My gaze stopped at the Lennoxes. They were here? Interesting.

What disturbed me was the fact that Mrs. Lennox wore a brown-and-white shrug around her neck. It was furry . . . and it reminded me of Big Boy.

***

As I walked out of the church, I made sure my path crossed with the Lennoxes'. Mrs. Lennox smiled, though the motion never reached her eyes. Instead, she pulled her shrug closer.

It was chilly outside, but it wasn't *that* chilly.

I paused, reining in all my "I'd rather be a frigid idiot than wear a fur" speeches. Instead, I nodded toward the atrocity around her shoulders. "Those colors . . . they remind me of something."

A touch of what appeared to be shock widened her eyes. She rubbed the gaudy and inhumane accessory. "The colors are nice, aren't they? This is a part of the new line we're debuting."

"You're heartless—" I started.

Before I could say anything, Chad pulled me away.

"You bred Big Boy, didn't you? Are those his puppies?" As the words left my mouth, I realized how absurd they sounded. But what other explanation could there be? People had said the Lennoxes didn't even like animals.

Chad tugged harder, leading me away from the gawking couple. That was probably better. The last thing I needed was to have a war of words here at church. Especially in front of my mother. Not to mention the commentary Aunt Yori might offer up in the process.

Anger burned inside me, though. How could people be so cruel and heartless? I just didn't understand it.

When we left church, the sky was a glorious blue with not a cloud in sight. I gulped in some fresh air, trying to calm down. But I couldn't get that shrug out of my mind.

"Should we call her Cruella?" Chad asked.

I frowned. "It appears. Maybe that's why Big Boy doesn't want to be caught. He's afraid he'll be next."

"It would be pretty extreme for someone to do this,

don't you think?"

I shrugged. "They inherited the company. Maybe they want to try something new and innovative in order to make a name for themselves."

I climbed into the driver's side, needing to focus my thoughts. Driving would do that, and Chad didn't mind if I was behind the wheel. Part of me wished we were driving back home right now. The other part of me still wanted more answers, more confirmations that something was still wrong.

We were supposed to eat a light lunch, and then tonight a few friends were coming over so we could eat the food from the ceremony-that-wasn't. My parents had already paid the caterer, and there were gobs of food in the garage fridge, apparently.

"Hard to believe the weekend is almost over, isn't it?" I asked. I felt like I'd been here a month with everything that had happened.

"Yeah, I guess there's a big job lined up for tomorrow. Gabby's going to need a hand."

"I figured we'd leave after dinner. That will put us getting back around midnight. Does that work?"

"Sounds fine. I'm just sorry things didn't work out for your parents."

I frowned, remembering how disastrous this weekend had been. "Me, too."

We had to go home and clean up the mess Big Boy had made in the backyard last night. It was going to be a dirty job, and I couldn't easily imagine my parents, their doctor friends, or Sharo helping.

As I drove, Chad played on his phone beside me.

"Those outfits your parents are collecting are pricey. Like crazy pricey. What did your dad say? More than $10,000? It looks like some of those others are worth close to $5,000."

"They only have value if people are willing to pay."

"I never saw your parents as the type to collect clothes, of all things. Maybe coins or stamps or artwork. But clothing?"

I shrugged. "You got me. I didn't see this coming either. Maybe my parents are having a midlife crisis."

"Sure enough, look at this. It's Dolly Parton wearing that dress that's in your parents' house."

I glanced over. Something about the outfit struck me. What was it?

I swerved my eyes back to the road. I couldn't let my gaze linger on the picture too long.

But as I thought about the leather number I'd seen in my parents' house, I realized the naughty-looking slit was on the wrong side.

Had my parents bought a counterfeit? Was the photo a mirror image, reversing the look of the dress? Or was I reading too much into this?

I'd been doing a lot of reading into things lately.

My parents had already had a miserable weekend. To bring something like this up seemed to only be inviting more tension. Besides, if the dress was fake or not, it made them happy. Maybe ignorance truly was bliss.

CHAPTER 23

Before we got out of the van, Chad pulled me toward him and planted a kiss on my lips.

"What was that for?" I asked.

"It's one reason I'll be happy to get home. At least I can act like your husband and not some unwanted boyfriend."

"Isn't *unwanted* strong?"

"Your aunt Yori wanted to fix you up with the priest," Chad reminded me.

"Well, there was that." I couldn't deny it.

"Are you still planning on telling your parents?"

At the mere mention of it, my shoulders tightened with subconscious anxiety. "They've had such a bad weekend."

"Sierra . . ."

I raised a hand to stop him before he continued with that thought. "But I will before we leave."

At least I still wouldn't be at the top of my parents' bad list. As long as my brother didn't show up; he was their biggest disappointment at the moment. My plan, as of right now, was to announce my news right before I left. I'd drop the bomb and walk away unharmed for the most part.

When we walked into the kitchen — we were the last ones to arrive back at the house — Aunt Yori stood in the middle of the kitchen.

"I have an announcement!" she yelled.

Everyone gathered around her. She held something in her hands, but I couldn't make out exactly what it was because she fluttered her arms around.

"I'd like to tell everyone something very important," she continued.

We all quieted.

She raised her hand higher, her timing and captive hold of the audience around her Hollywood worthy. "I'd like to announce that . . . I'm pregnant!"

"Yori!" my mother scolded. "Stop being so foolish."

A flurry of whispers, giggles, and gasps went around the room like the crowd doing the wave at a baseball game.

"You heard the priest talk about it today. Abraham and Sarah." Aunt Yori waved the item in her hands. "You can have a baby at my age. I knew it!"

That's when I realized what it was.

A pregnancy test.

She must have found the box I'd accidentally brought in this morning. I covered my gaping mouth with my hand.

"Put that down, Yori. Speaking of which, maybe you should lie down for a little while. There's been a lot going on this weekend." My mom led her toward the hallway where her bedroom was.

Silence remained for a moment. Finally, I pointed to the stairs. "I'm going to go get changed before lunch."

"Good idea," my sister concurred.

"Right," Greg said.

Everyone scattered. I pulled on some jeans and a long-sleeved T-shirt. I needed to be ready to clean up outside. Ms. B. couldn't clean it all up on her own. It was the least I could do before I left.

When I came back downstairs, the doorbell rang.

Ms. Blankenship answered and let out a long, loud gasp.

I peered beyond her, worst-case scenarios flashing in my mind.

The police?

A bomb?

Another bone?

Unfortunately, it was none of those things.

It was my brother.

***

While everyone else stayed inside and treated my brother like long-lost royalty, Chad and I slipped outside to work. My sister offered to go with us, but my mom insisted she stay inside and take it easy, which was strange, but I didn't have time to think about it too much.

I'd give my family their moment and their little

reunion. It was better if I kept myself busy. Because, with the one simple act of my perfect brother returning home, things suddenly looked bad for me.

I only had a few hours to fess up that I was married. And my scapegoat was no longer viable. Everyone seemed happy to see him, even Sharo—which I thought was weird.

"Your brother isn't who I expected," Chad said, pulling the hose out.

I nodded. "Yeah, he's . . . he's my brother. Kenji Nakamura, world-class plastic surgeon."

Somehow, he'd returned home, and now my mom was all smiles. While I was glad she'd cheered up, I just wished she was as proud of me as she was my brother.

I had to keep my thoughts on something else, so I kept thinking about that necklace as I picked up muddy chairs and Chad hosed them off. It had to be significant. I just didn't see how it wasn't.

I supposed the most obvious answer was that it belonged to Mrs. Lennox. She seemed like the fashion-connoisseur type with her furs and designer clothes. Had the necklace been hers? If it was, had Big Boy eaten it in conjunction with Winnie dying, or was it just a terrible coincidence?

"I wanted to come outside and help my favorite little sister."

I looked up and saw my brother there. Really? He was going to get dirty. He'd rolled up the sleeves of his baby-blue button-up shirt and taken his tie off, and was apparently willing to sacrifice his designer pants.

My brother was on the shorter side, but he carried himself like he was a giant. He had a magnetic smile, thick, perfect hair, and a bit of a playboy flair. His practice was located outside of New York City, and every time he posted to social media, he was in expensive-looking bars surrounded by beautiful women. He'd been married once, only for a year, but long enough to have a little girl who was now fourteen. His ex-wife had custody, and I rarely got to see her anymore.

I also thought it was strange that he seemed to know Sharo. How had the two of them met? Or did my brother simply know everyone?

Chad nodded toward the house. "You know what? Maybe I'll go help get the hair dye out of the rug and shower curtain."

Aunt Yori had decided to dye her hair red and purple, just like one of her favorite anime characters. If anyone could get those stains out, it was Chad. But I knew what he was really doing was giving my brother and me some time alone.

My brother watched Chad walk away while straightening another chair. "You know, if his hair was a little shorter, I do think he has the facial structure of a Ken doll."

"Thanks . . . I think."

"You look good, Sierra. You have a glow about you that I haven't seen before."

"Life is good. I can't complain."

"So, tell me about everything I've missed this weekend."

He probably had no idea the can of worms he was opening. I spilled everything. And I do mean everything—except for my marriage.

"So, you think the dead body is somehow connected with Mom and Dad?"

I shrugged. "I think it's somehow connected with what's going on this weekend. I just don't know how yet." I paused. "By the way, do you know Sharo?"

He nodded, setting up the last chair. "That's right. She's into the New York social scene, to say the least. Last I heard, she got divorced from her filthy-rich husband—another reminder to me why I never want to get married. When the divorce happens, the ex always tries to leech all your money."

So that was his reason? I wondered if Mom and Dad knew that. "A socialite wedding planner, huh? The guests here just keep getting stranger and stranger, starting with our direct bloodline: Aunt Yori."

He chuckled.

Some of the tulle had blown over the back gate. Once I picked that up, we'd be done. I stepped toward the woods, briefly wondering if my buddy Big Boy would reappear.

I glanced down at the other side of the fence and paused. It was a bowl of dog food.

And there was a white, powdery substance

sprinkled on top of it.

CHAPTER 24

I plopped the dog bowl on my kitchen counter. Everyone stopped talking and turned to look at me.

"Anyone want to fess up?" I asked.

"Is that Cocoa Puffs? I love Cocoa Puffs." Aunt Yori started to reach for one when I jerked the bowl back.

"It's dog food, Aunt Yori." *Poisoned dog food.*

She frowned. "It still looks quite tasty."

"Yori!" my mother chastised.

"What are you doing with that bowl, Sierra?" my dad asked. His eyebrow twitched.

"I found it outside."

Greg shrugged. "So someone's trying to feed the dog. What's the big deal?"

"The big deal is that there's poison on top of this food." I pointed to the white powder coating.

A couple of people gasped.

"How can you be sure?" my brother asked. He'd followed me inside, barely keeping up.

"I'm not one hundred percent positive, but I'm nearly certain. I'm definitely not going to test it."

My sister averted her gaze for a moment before raising her hand. "I left the food out there. I hated to see the dog starve. But I did not put the white powder on top."

"You like Big Boy?" Surprise dripped in my voice.

Reina nodded. "Of course I do. I'm a vet. I love animals, and I don't want to see anything happen to the dog."

"You shouldn't be handling poison," my mom told my sister.

"I didn't!" she insisted.

"So who put the poison on top?" I mused aloud.

A chorus of "I don't know," "Beats me," "No idea" followed.

"It could be a mold," Sharo offered.

I glanced at her. "Why would you think that?"

She shrugged. "Just a guess."

"Reina, you should sit down. You're looking tired," my mom said.

"I'm fine," Reina insisted. "I've never seen you so concerned about me."

I stood up. "Does anyone here besides me care that someone is trying to kill that dog?"

No one said anything.

I shook my head. "You know what? I need to take a little walk and cool off for a minute. Excuse me."

"I'll go with her," Chad said behind me.

We walked silently down the road for a minute until finally Chad said, "What are you doing?"

"Cooling off."

"That's all?"

"That's all right now."

"You seem angry."

"Someone's trying to kill an innocent dog. Of course I'm angry."

"You know that Mrs. Jericho already confessed to accidentally killing Winnie, right?"

"I just can't buy it. Something's not right." I veered off the street toward the Lennoxes' house. "Besides, someone else tried to kill that dog, and this family is my best bet."

"You're just going to charge there and ask them?"

"I don't know, but I can't let this slide."

"Sierra . . ." Concern filled Chad's voice.

"It's even about more than murder or poisoning a dog. This is about my job with Paws and Furballs. The Lennoxes are the owners of East Coast Fur Traders. I need to explain to them who I am."

"You think that will scare them? It will probably just annoy them. You need to think this through, Sierra."

"I'll tell them that I'm going to do an expose on the company. I'll give them fair warning. I can be civil about these things."

"You *can* be, that's correct. You just seem emotionally charged right now."

"It's called *passionate*." I stopped and turned to him. "Don't talk me out of this. I need to at least speak my piece. If I get out of control, you can reel me in. Okay?"

Chad kissed my forehead. "Okay."

Some of my tension subsided. Chad had a way of doing that.

I rang the doorbell, reviewing everything in my mind. The fur industry was inhumane. There were better ways of doing things. Did Big Boy have something to do with this? Or was I reading too much into things?

Mrs. Lennox answered. Her eyes widened when she saw me. "You. Again." She stared at me coldly. "What can I do for you?"

"Mrs. Lennox, there's something you should know," I started. "I'm the director of Paws and Furballs. I adamantly oppose what your company does. I find it deplorable how animals are treated—"

"You're with Paws and Furballs?" Mrs. Lennox asked, her voice filled with surprise.

I nodded, halfway annoyed. "That's correct."

"I love Paws and Furballs." She emphasized the words by placing a hand on her heart.

I blinked. "What?"

She nodded. "It's true. I was considering becoming one of your supporters."

"What?" I repeated. This was not how I expected this conversation to go.

"You know we just took over the company six months ago, right? Reggie's father passed away, and Reggie's running the business now. I've never been a supporter of this industry."

"I thought you hated animals?"

She shook her head. "No, I don't hate animals. I mean, I'm not a fan of dogs. I really should have gotten something small that would sit on my lap. Horace just isn't a great fit with our family. He'd rather be tromping through the woods."

"Okay . . . so you didn't breed him and use his puppies for your shrug?"

She gaped. "What? No. Never. I would never do that. It's illegal in the United States anyway. Why in the world . . . ? Never mind." She shook her head.

"That what about the shrug you wore today? And the new product you're launching that everyone's going to love? And the fights you and your husband have been having?"

"Wow. You are thorough, aren't you? The shrug I wore this morning is a fake fur."

"What?" I tried not to screech.

"Yes, we're changing the direction of the company, and we're going to be the leading provider of fake furs in the country. Didn't it look real? I must admit, when I saw Horace, I thought his coat was gorgeous. The piece I wore today was inspired by him."

"I feel so stupid," I muttered. I didn't say stuff like that very often. But it was true. I'd jumped to some major conclusions. "But with the blood—"

"My husband really does get nosebleeds."

"The bloody tarp—"

"We just stained our deck."

"The fight neighbors overheard you having—"

"Running a business is stressful."

I shook my head. "I'm sorry."

"Listen, don't worry about it. Better a concerned citizen than an apathetic one. Do you have a card?" she asked.

I reached into my pocket and pulled one out. "Here you go."

"Great. I'll be in touch. I really think we can work together and revolutionize the fur industry. I want that to be my legacy. No more animals involved in the process. It can happen. There's amazing technology out there that can imitate real fur."

I felt dumbfounded as I turned back to Chad. He shrugged, a bit of a glint in his eyes. Like a smart man, he kept his mouth shut, though.

"Let's get home," I mumbled. "We've got to have dinner and start packing, I suppose."

CHAPTER 25

As I shoved a shirt into my suitcase, my mind turned over everything I'd learned. There was something about me that just hated to leave things unfinished, and this whole mystery felt like it had too many loose ends.

The most glaring reason was: if Mrs. Jericho was in jail, someone else had tried to poison Big Boy.

Someone who didn't know that Mrs. Jericho had been arrested, perhaps?

Someone who still thought he or she might be discovered? Or who thought that incriminating evidence still might be churning in Big Boy's stomach?

Who might that be? It had to be someone who wasn't here last night when the whole arrest had gone down.

My mind ran through the possibilities.

And I stopped on one person.

The thought hit me like a slap in the face.

No. Could it be? Clues flashed in my mind with striking clarity. My original theories had been totally wrong. But this one could work.

It could be right!

But how would I prove it?

I could do what the archerfish did. When they spotted the enemy, they shot them with spit to throw them off balance, and then went in for the kill.

In other words, I could smoke this person out. But in order to do so, I'd need my parents' help.

That thought caused a brick to form in my stomach. But I had to give it a shot.

Because, if I didn't, a killer might get away with murder.

***

I don't know how I convinced them, but my parents agreed to go along with my plan. However, if I had to guess, they were terrible actors, which was a problem, since my whole plan was dependent on them being convincing. In fact, I couldn't even fathom them giving this a chance and selling the whole idea. But this was all I had at the moment.

We were going to have a dinner together tonight in lieu of the ceremony that didn't happen yesterday. But first, my parents wanted to say a few words. The doorbell had just rung again, and according to my calculations, that meant everyone was here.

I glanced at my mom and dad. "You ready to do this?"

"If you're sure, Sierra." Worry lines formed around my mom's eyes.

I wasn't sure, but I wasn't about to tell her that. If I didn't have faith in my plan, how would anyone else? "This isn't just about Winnie or Big Boy. This is personal," I reminded them.

"I hope you're right," my dad said. His eyebrow twitched.

We walked downstairs together. All the guests were waiting in the living room. I grabbed a goblet of water from the kitchen and tapped a fork against it to get everyone's attention.

"I wanted to say something before we all sit down to eat," I started, praying I wouldn't start perspiring. "I am so thrilled to announce that my parents have graciously agreed to donate three of the valuable costumes they've been collecting to Paws and Furballs, one of the leading animal rights organizations in the country."

My father nodded and stepped toward me. "We knew when we originally bought the outfits that one day we'd like to donate them for a good cause. Two of the clothing sets are associated with upcoming movies that will be releasing. We expect a sizable donation to come from this."

"An auctioneer is coming to pick them up in an hour," I continued. "I just wanted to thank my parents, not only for organizing this celebration this weekend, but also for their generous donation."

A ripple of applause traveled through the room.

My mom joined us at the front of the crowd. "If you

would, we also have butterflies we brought in for the service yesterday that still need to be released. I'd be pleased if you'd all join us outside to perform this symbolic act of love and freedom."

I had to give my parents credit; they'd sold it. They did have a few tricks up their sleeves.

I followed the crowd onto the deck, but Chad hung back. I nodded at him, giving him the signal to go. I'd hang out for a minute before circling back inside and joining him.

I just hoped all of this didn't blow up. That the right person took the bait.

I'd organized many shenanigans in my life, but the stakes seemed especially high on this one.

While everyone else watched the butterflies flutter in the air—another practice I didn't approve of, in case anyone was wondering—I slipped back inside. I didn't have much time.

Just as I rounded the corner, I practically tackled someone approaching on the other side. I sucked in a deep breath, fear causing my already heightened emotions to skyrocket.

My breathing slowed when I saw a familiar face. Dr. Moto.

"Sierra, are you okay?" He peered at me, concern across his fine features.

I nodded, my heart still stampeding out of control. "I'm fine. Just running up to the bathroom for a minute."

"While I have you here, I wanted to say thank you."

My throat squeezed as I realized the minutes were ticking away. I tried to look casual as I paused against the wall. "Thank me? For what?"

"I understand that Winnie may have forged my signature on one of the documents at the office. I consider myself a careful man, but in the future I will be even more careful."

"How'd you know?"

"Shaunda told me. After your talk with her, she felt compelled to come forward. Thank you, Sierra." With that, he patted me on the back and continued outside.

As soon as he was out of sight, I ducked down the back hallway and darted up the stairs. I crept inside the collectible room, pushed aside my fears as the darkness surrounded me, and rushed toward the closet. My throat went dry as I opened the door and slid inside.

"Chad?" I whispered, prickles racing up my skin.

"It's me," he whispered back with a ghostly voice.

I elbowed him in the stomach—or so I thought.

"Ow! That was my nose."

"Sorry about that." I settled back comfortably on my knees, making sure I was sitting in a position to easily spring but also not lose my balance and alert anyone of my presence.

"Do you think this is going to work?" Chad asked.

"We can only hope." I'd never done something like this before, so I was by no means an expert.

We sat in silence for a few minutes, waiting.

My heart rammed into my chest, echoing all the way to my ears. It was only offset by my aching bones and the slight feeling of nausea that had been lingering in my gut since I arrived at my parents' place.

I checked the time on my phone. There were only ten more minutes until the "appraiser" was supposed to be here to pick up the outfits. That didn't give the culprit much time. If this person was going to strike, it had to be soon.

As soon as the thought entered my mind, I heard a creak.

I squeezed Chad's arm, then froze, listened, hardly even breathed.

There was a click. Then another creak, almost like . . . footsteps.

Someone was definitely in here!

I peered through the crack in the door. A penlight appeared across the room. I heard the sound of something zipping and then tugging. I couldn't tell much about what was going on, but I had a pretty good guess.

I waited until I thought I saw the Dolly Parton outfit leave the mannequin. That's when I knew I had her.

"Let's go!" I whispered.

Chad and I burst from the closet. I darted across the room and flipped the lights. As the dark dispersed, my suspicions were confirmed.

"Sharo," I rumbled. "Just as I suspected."

She froze mid-action, holding a black leather gown

in her hands—a black leather gown that looked just like the one on the mannequin. A double.

Her eyes widened. "I was just inspecting the dresses before the auction house came by."

"No, you're not. You're switching these outfits for counterfeits. You used to be a designer, which means you're probably a seamstress also. Those numbers I saw on your clipboard weren't itemized billing items. They were measurements for the gown. Dolly Parton's measurements, to be specific."

"Why would I do that?" Her expression looked a little too innocent—forcibly so.

"You're selling the real ones to fund your lifestyle, which has been in serious decline since your divorce. I looked it up and saw numerous articles featuring details. Prenups can be a real lemon. Or so I've heard."

She chuckled unconvincingly. "Those are some theories, but I don't know what you're talking about."

"I think you do. Winnie stumbled onto what you're doing, and you're the one who really killed her. Mrs. Jericho may have hit her with her car, but you finished her off. That's why there was mud on your tires also. It wasn't from the bakery. You went out in the woods searching for Big Boy. He found you after you killed Winnie, knew something was wrong, and tried to stop you. That's how he ended up eating your necklace. You knew that could be the smoking gun that would put you behind bars."

She stared at me another moment before bursting

into a run.

"After her!" I shouted. As if Chad didn't know.

We both sprinted toward the door. We had to catch her before she got away.

CHAPTER 26

We rushed down the stairs, but Sharo was four steps ahead of us. Even in high heels, that woman could run.

Everyone else was outside in the backyard, so there was no one to stop her. She dodged tables, knocked a lamp into our path, and ran toward the front door.

Her obstacles slowed us up enough that she was outside before we could hurdle the furniture. I hadn't anticipated Sharo would be faster than we were.

I jumped down the front steps in one leap. As soon as my feet hit the pavers, I pushed myself until my muscles strained. This was one pursuit I wasn't going to let up on.

She reached her car, and the first self-doubt hit me. What if she got away?

Just then, something caught my eye.

I turned in time to see Big Boy bound out of the woods and charge toward Sharo. Before I could say, "Save the animals!" Big Boy had Sharo pinned on the ground.

Sharo screamed and tried to get the dog to move. He wasn't going anywhere.

Just then, Detective Meadows pulled up with a screech and burst from her sedan. "Would someone like to explain what's going on here? I was just enjoying a *Longmire* marathon, so I hope this is important."

Yes, I'd called the detective first. Of course.

"I found Winnie's killer." I pointed to Sharo.

"Winnie's killer has already confessed," Detective Meadows said with a scowl.

"That's right. Please, get this beast off me. I'm innocent here." Sharo struggled against Big Boy, but she was no match to the dog's brute—and adorable—strength. Big Boy remained on top of her, his tongue hanging out and drool hitting Sharo squarely on the forehead.

"Did I mention how helpful those online articles were? Not only did they talk about her divorce, but they also mentioned that she liked to frequent some of the premiere auction houses—mostly for art. But that changed when she saw how much people—namely, my parents—were paying for those outfits of the stars. That's when a plan formed."

"Sounds like a lot of guesses to me," Sharo said.

By this time, everyone from the backyard had gathered around for the show. I had to step up my game here.

"You were never a wedding planner," I said, maybe with a touch of dramatic flair to my voice. "That much should have been obvious. I mean, what wedding planner doesn't know what order people are being seated? You offered your services just so you could get into the house and switch out the real outfits for fake ones."

"That's just speculation," Sharo mumbled, moaning as more doggy drool hit her cheek. "Now will someone get this dog off me?"

No one moved, including Big Boy.

"You were in the process of sneaking one of the dresses into your car on Wednesday night—when you knew my parents would be gone at bridge—when Winnie came stumbling into the yard," I said, pacing like a cocky defense attorney in court. "You knew she'd seen the dress, and you couldn't risk being caught. That's when you thwacked her—I'm not sure with what, maybe your purse—and killed her. You didn't know what to do, so you drug her into the woods."

"Prove it!" Sharo snarled.

I was on a roll. "Big Boy swallowed your necklace. The symbol on the pendant was the same one that's on your stationery. I saw it that day I was looking through my parents' bills. You've been trying to catch the dog since that happened. You put poison on his food because you knew you'd eventually be discovered if the police got their hands on that necklace."

"You don't know what you're talking about."

"If you're innocent, you won't mind us checking out your trunk, correct?" the detective said. "That would clear everything up."

"Not without a warrant!"

A sure sign of guilt, I couldn't help but think.

"If you go upstairs, you'll see a knockoff of at least three of the collectible outfits that my parents own. How can you explain that, Sharo?"

I stared down on her. Big Boy seemed to pick up on my cues and began growling.

Sharo screamed. "Okay, okay. I admit it! I was going to switch out the outfits. No one was supposed to get hurt. I just needed some money. My good-for-nothing ex-husband wrote an ironclad prenup. I have an image to live up to!"

"Wouldn't people know these outfits didn't rightfully belong to you anyway?" I asked.

She sneered. "I have a buyer in Qatar lined up. I'm meeting him tonight. I was supposed to switch out the outfits at the ceremony yesterday, but everything got canceled."

"Who is this buyer?" Detective Meadows asked.

Something lit in her gaze—the realization that she had the chance to frame someone else. "He's the real guilty one! Arrest him! I'll give you his name, his address, anything you need. He was going to smuggle them out of the country!"

"Why leave Aunt Yori in the closet, though?"

Sharo didn't say anything, but her scowl said plenty. "Your crazy aunt walked in while I was getting some measurements. Thankfully everyone already thinks she's a few stitches short of being held together.

Otherwise, if someone had actually believed her, this whole operation would have been toast."

Behind me, Aunt Yori started singing, "Viva Las Vegas."

That's why she'd been talking about Vegas! The costumes had triggered the thought of stars onstage, glamour, and sequins. It was all making sense now.

Detective Meadows took Sharo's elbow and pulled her off the ground. Big Boy stepped off, looking pleased with himself as he continued to pant and looked unfazed by what had just happened. "You have the right to remain silent . . ."

As she was leading Sharo toward her car, the detective paused. "Good job, Mrs. Davis."

The blood drained from my face as my shining moment turned into a nightmare.

CHAPTER 27

"Who's Mrs. Davis? There's no Mrs. Davis here," my mom muttered.

Speculation fluttered through the crowd. I glanced at Chad, and he shrugged. This was all me. My mess. My moment to spill the truth.

I held my head high. "Yes, I am Mrs. Davis. Chad and I are married. We tied the knot a couple of months ago."

A collective gasp sounded through the crowd.

My mother stepped forward, her mouth gaping open. "Married? How could you have not told me?"

"Because I knew you wouldn't approve. I wanted to enjoy my wedding day, not be worried about making you unhappy." I braced myself for her reaction. I expected a reprimand, at the least; anger, at the most.

"I admit that I made some mistakes when you were growing up. If we could go back, I would do things differently. But all I want is for you to be happy, Sierra." She sounded surprisingly calm and in control. "I don't always realize that what I consider to be best for you isn't what you consider the most worthy use of your time, and I apologize for that."

"Really?" I was speechless. Truly.

"I'll fight for you tooth and nail, Sierra, but in the end the decisions you make are yours, and I must accept them." She paused, her eyes misting a moment. "When I thought I had cancer, you could say my perspective changed."

"Cancer?" My heart felt like it stopped.

She glanced at my father. "I found a lump on my abdomen."

"What?" I still couldn't believe it.

"It was biopsied and benign. But still, it made us both realize how very easily we could be in the same position that the many patients we treat are in. There are very few guarantees in life. None of us knows how much time we've been given."

I glanced at my dad, tears welling in my eyes. "I can't believe it. What if . . . ?"

He nodded solemnly. "We didn't want to tell you because we thought you'd worry too much, especially since you're so focused on your career."

"That's why you're doing the vow ceremony, isn't it? And the costume collecting and bridge games. It's all because of that. They're changes that only a possible dance with death can bring about." Everything suddenly made sense.

"I started to tell you upstairs in the Collector's Room yesterday, but we got interrupted," my father said.

I'd been trying to protect her; all the while my mom

had been trying to protect me, as well. Maybe there were too many secrets in this family, too many good intentions hidden in the glare of past mistakes.

Without thinking, I threw my arms around my mom. As much as we didn't see eye to eye, I didn't want anything to happen to my parents. Maybe I'd wanted them to change just as much as they'd wanted me to change.

As surprising as it was to me, my parents were real people with real emotions. In their own ways, they cared about me. There were some things we'd never see eye to eye on, but with the realization that they wouldn't live forever came the desire to try harder, to make the most of the time we had.

We pulled apart, and I sniffled again. Big Boy even barked, as if to show his approval. But I wasn't done; there was one more thing I had to say, one more motivation to build bridges.

I grabbed Chad's hand and held it tight. "I guess you should all know that not only is Chad my husband, but we're going to have a baby."

Chad's eyes widened. "What?"

I nodded, my throat tight and more tears flowing down my cheeks. "It's true. I'm pregnant." My hand instinctively went to my belly.

"What . . .? How . . . ?" Chad looked stupefied.

"I'd wondered for a week or two. I saw those pregnancy tests this morning and decided on a whim to take one. To my surprise, it came back as positive."

"Wow," Chad muttered. He pulled me into a hug and didn't let go for a long time.

I hoped that meant he was happy.

"I thought it was Reina," my mom muttered. "I found the test in the trash."

"Is that why you've been acting so weird around me?" Reina asked. "I thought you were going crazy."

My mom nodded. "I know you want kids. I thought it had finally happened."

Reina shook her head. "No, Mark and I don't want kids, actually. We're quite content with our four-legged children. I didn't think you'd understand."

"Sounds like there's a lot of misunderstanding going on," my dad said.

We all hugged it out before my mom turned back to me. "Congratulations, Sierra. I'm going to be a grandmother again! I can't believe it."

"I say this calls for a celebration," my dad said.

"It's a beautiful day." I raised my hand to display the marvelous blue sky. "Why don't we have the renewal ceremony? Just the people who are here?"

"I like that idea," my mom said, wrapping her arm around my father's waist.

Big Boy barked again.

My mom and dad even laughed this time. Surprisingly, my mom leaned toward the dog and patted his head. "You really saved the day, troublemaker."

"He's probably going to be looking for a new

home," I started. "I don't think the Lennoxes have time for him."

"Maybe we should get a dog," my father said.

I raised my eyebrows in surprise. Had I heard him correctly?

My mom obviously felt the same way, because she turned to him with her lips slightly apart. "Are you serious?"

He shrugged. "The collection-of-iconic-clothing venture didn't work out very well."

"We've never had a dog," my mom said.

"People with dogs are proven to live longer, healthier lives," I offered. "And you will be retiring soon."

"He's certainly been a lifesaver this weekend, in spite of everything." My mom squatted down beside him. "It would be nice to have a watchdog. Maybe I'll talk to the Lennoxes and see how they feel about this pup staying here."

I grinned. "I think it's a great idea."

"But what about the costumes we've already purchased?" My mom stood back up. "What will we ever do with those hideously overpriced pieces of clothing?"

"How about we really do donate the money to Paws and Furballs? It's the least we could do for our youngest daughter." He turned toward me. "How's that sound to you, Mrs. Davis?"

I nodded. "That would be wonderful. We could

really use the funding."

"Consider it done, then," my dad said. "Now, let me go make a few phone calls and see if the priest is available to come out."

I smiled as I watched him walk away. Maybe coming home hadn't been so bad after all.

Ms. B. squeezed through the crowd. "Congratulations, Sierra. I just know you're a wonderful wife and that you're going to be a wonderful mother. I'm so happy for you."

"Thank you, Ms. B. That means a lot."

She kissed my cheeks and then scurried back toward the house.

When everyone cleared away, Chad pulled me close.

"A baby, huh?" he asked.

I nodded. "I guess that explains why I've been feeling so nauseous lately. How's that news make you feel?"

"Like I'm walking on sunshine. I cannot wait to see what the future holds for us, Sierra."

"For better or for worse, right?"

He grinned. "For better or for worse. But I have a feeling there's a lot of 'better' waiting for us."

He planted a tender kiss on my lips, and I suddenly realized that this trip home wasn't a bad idea after all.

###

Look for these books in the Squeaky Clean series:

Hazardous Duty (Book 1)

On her way to completing a degree in forensic science, Gabby St. Claire drops out of school and starts her own crime scene cleaning business. "Yeah, that's me," she says, "a crime scene cleaner. People waiting in line behind me who strike up conversations always regret it."

When a routine cleaning job uncovers a murder weapon the police overlooked, she realizes that the wrong person is in jail. But the owner of the weapon is a powerful foe . . . and willing to do anything to keep Gabby quiet.

With the help of her new neighbor, Riley Thomas, a man whose life and faith fascinate her, Gabby plays the detective to make sure the right person is put behind bars. Can Riley help her before another murder occurs?

Suspicious Minds (Book 2)

In this smart and suspenseful sequel to *Hazardous Duty*, crime scene cleaner Gabby St. Claire finds herself stuck doing mold remediation to pay the bills. But her first day on the job, she uncovers a surprise in the crawlspace of a dilapidated home: Elvis, dead as a doornail and still wearing his blue suede shoes. How could she possibly keep her nose out of a case like this?

It Came Upon a Midnight Crime (Book 2.5, a Novella)

Someone is intent on destroying the true meaning of Christmas — at least, destroying anything that hints of it. All around crime scene cleaner Gabby St. Claire's hometown, anything pointing to Jesus as the "reason for the season" is being sabotaged. The crimes become more twisted as dismembered body parts are found at the vandalisms. Who would go to such great lengths to dampen the joy and hope of Christ's birthday? Someone's determined to destroy Christmas . . . but Gabby St. Claire is just as determined to find the Grinch and let peace on earth and goodwill to men prevail.

Organized Grime (Book 3)

Gabby St. Claire knows her best friend, Sierra, isn't guilty of killing three people in what appears to be an eco-terrorist attack. But Sierra has disappeared, her only contact a frantic phone call to Gabby proclaiming that she's being hunted. Gabby is determined to prove her friend is innocent and to keep her alive. While trying to track down the real perpetrator, Gabby notices a disturbing trend at the crime scenes she's cleaning, one that ties random crimes together — and points to Sierra as the guilty party. Just what has her friend gotten herself into?

Dirty Deeds (Book 4)

"Promise me one thing. No snooping. Just for one week."

Gabby St. Claire knows that her fiancé's request is a simple one that she should be able to honor. After all, Riley's law school reunion and attorneys' conference at a hoity-toity resort is a chance for them to get away from the mysteries Gabby often finds herself involved in as a crime scene cleaner. The weeklong trip is a chance for them to be "normal," a word that leaves a bad taste in Gabby's mouth.

But Gabby finds herself alone for endless hours while Riley is busy with legal workshops. Then one of Riley's old friends goes missing, and Gabby suspects one of Riley's buddies might be behind the disappearance. When the missing woman's mom asks Gabby for help, how can she say no?

Secrets abound. Frankly, Gabby even has some of her own. When the dirty truth comes out, the revelations put everything in jeopardy — relationships, trusts, and even lives.

The Scum of All Fears (Book 5)

"I'll get out, and I'll get even."

Gabby St. Claire is back to crime-scene cleaning, at least temporarily. With her business partner on his honeymoon, she needs help after a weekend killing spree fills up her work docket. She quickly realizes she has bigger problems than finding temporary help.

A serial killer her fiancé, a former prosecutor, put behind bars has escaped. His last words to Riley were: *I'll get out, and I'll get even.* Pictures of Gabby are found in the man's prison cell, and Riley fears the sadistic madman has Gabby in his sights.

Gabby tells herself there's no way the Scum River Killer will make it across the country from California to Virginia without being caught. But then messages are left for Gabby at crime scenes, and someone keeps slipping in and out of her apartment.

When Gabby's temporary assistant disappears, Gabby must figure out who's behind these crimes. The search for answers becomes darker when Gabby realizes she's dealing with a criminal who's more than evil. He's truly the scum of the earth, and he'll do anything to make Gabby and Riley's lives a living nightmare.

To Love, Honor, and Perish (Book 6)
How could God let this happen?

Crime scene cleaner Gabby St. Claire can't stop asking the question. Just when her life is on the right track, the unthinkable happens. Gabby's fiancé, Riley Thomas, is shot and remains in life-threatening condition only a week before their wedding.

Gabby is determined to figure out who pulled the trigger, even if investigating puts her own life at risk. But as she digs deeper into the facts surrounding the case, she discovers secrets better left alone. Doubts arise in her mind and the one man with answers is on death's doorstep.

An old foe from the past returns and tests everything Gabby is made of — physically, mentally, and spiritually. Will her soul survive the challenges ahead? Or will everything she's worked for be destroyed?

Mucky Streak (Book 7)

After her last encounter with a serial killer, Gabby St. Claire feels her life is smeared with the stain of tragedy. Between the exhaustion of trying to get her fiancé back on his feet, routine night terrors, and potential changes looming on the horizon, she needs a respite from the mire of life.

At the encouragement of her friends, she takes on a short-term gig as a private investigator: a cold case that's eluded investigators for ten years. The mass murder of a wealthy family seems impossible to solve but quickly gets interesting as Gabby brings more clues to light. Add to the mix a flirtatious client, travels to an exciting new city, and some quirky — albeit temporary — new sidekicks, and things get really complicated.

With every new development, Gabby prays that what she's calling her "mucky streak" will end and the future will become clear. But every answer she uncovers leads her closer to danger — both for her life and for her heart.

<u>Coming Soon:</u>
Broom and Gloom (Book 9)

The Sierra Files

Pounced (Book 1)

Sierra is used to fighting for the lives of innocent creatures. But when a killer puts the lives of her own cats on the line, her crusade becomes personal.

Animal rights activist Sierra Nakamura never expected to stumble upon the dead body of a coworker while out filming a project. She definitely never expected to get involved in the investigation. But when someone threatens to kill her cats unless she hands over the "information," she becomes more bristly than an angry feline.

Making matters worse is the fact that her cats — and the investigation — are driving a wedge between her and her boyfriend Chad. With every answer she uncovers, old hurts rise to the surface and test her beliefs.

Saving her cats just might mean ruining everything else in her life. In the fight for survival, one thing is certain: It's either pounce or be pounced.

The Gabby St. Claire Diaries (a Tween Mystery series)

(This series follows the life of a young Gabby St. Claire and is perfect for readers ages 10 and up)

The Curtain Call Caper (Book 1)

Is a ghost haunting the Oceanside Middle School auditorium? What else could explain the disasters surrounding the school play—everything from missing scripts to a falling spotlight and damaged props?

All seventh grader Gabby St. Claire has dreamed about is being a part of her school's musical. But a series of unfortunate events threatens to shut down the whole production. While trying to track down the culprit and save her fifteen minutes of fame, she also has to manage impossible teachers, cliques, her dysfunctional family, and a secret she can't even tell her best friend.

Will Gabby figure out who or what is sabotaging the show . . . or will it be curtains for her and the rest of the cast?

The Disappearing Dog Dilemma (Book 2)

Why are dogs from all over town disappearing? Who could be taking them from their loving families?

When two friends ask seventh grader Gabby St. Claire

for her help in finding their missing canines, Gabby decides to unleash her sleuthing skills to sniff out whoever's behind the act. But time management and relationships get tricky as worrisome weather, a part-time job, and a new crush interfere with Gabby's investigation.

Will her determination crack the case? Or will shadowy villains, a penchant for overcommitting, and even her own heart put her in the doghouse?

The Bundled Bike Burglaries (Book 3)

Stolen bikes and a long-forgotten time capsule leave one amateur sleuth baffled and busy.

Seventh grader Gabby St. Claire is determined to bring a bike burglar to justice—and not just because mean girl Donabell Bullock is strong-arming her into it. But each new clue brings its own set of trouble. As if that's not enough to handle, Gabby finds evidence of a decades-old murder within the contents of the time capsule, but no one seems to take her seriously.

As her investigation heats up, will Gabby's knack for being in the wrong place at the wrong time with the wrong people crack the case? Or will it prove hazardous to her health?

Other Books by Christy Barritt

Squeaky Clean Mysteries:
#1 Hazardous Duty
#2 Suspicious Minds
#2.5 It Came Upon a Midnight Crime
#3 Organized Grime
#4 Dirty Deeds
#5 The Scum of All Fears
#6 To Love, Honor, and Perish
#7 Mucky Streak
#8 Foul Play
#9 Broom and Gloom (coming December 2014)

The Sierra Files
#1 Pounced
#2 Hunted

The Gabby St. Claire Diaries (a Tween Mystery series)
#1 The Curtain Call Caper
#2 The Disappearing Dog Dilemma
#3 The Bungled Bike Burglaries

Holly Anna Paladin Mysteries
#1 Random Acts of Murder
#2 Random Acts of Malice (coming in 2015)

Suburban Sleuth Mysteries:
#1 Death of the Couch Potato's Wife

Stand-alone Romantic-Suspense:
Keeping Guard
The Last Target
Race Against Time
Ricochet
Key Witness
Lifeline
High-Stakes Holiday Reunion
Desperate Measures
Hidden Agenda (coming in March 2015)

Standalone Romantic Mystery:
The Good Girl

Suspense:
The Trouble with Perfect
Home Before Dark
Dubiosity (coming in January 2015)

Nonfiction:
Changed: True Stories of Finding God through
Christian Music
The Novel in Me: The Beginner's Guide to Writing and
Publishing a Novel

About the Author:

USA Today has called Christy Barritt's books "scary, funny, passionate, and quirky."

Christy writes both mystery and romantic suspense novels that are clean with underlying messages of faith. Her books have won the Daphne du Maurier Award for Excellence in Suspense and Mystery, have been twice nominated for the Romantic Times' Reviewers' Choice Award, and have finaled for both a Carol Award and Foreword Magazine's Book of the Year.

She's married to her Prince Charming, a man who thinks she's hilarious--but only when she's not trying to be. Christy's a self-proclaimed klutz, an avid music lover who's known for spontaneously bursting into song, and a road trip aficionado.

When she's not working or spending time with her family, she enjoys singing, playing the guitar, and exploring small, unsuspecting towns where people have no idea how accident prone she is.

Find Christy online at:
www.christybarritt.com
www.facebook.com/christybarritt
www.twitter.com/cbarritt

Sign up for Christy's newsletter to get information on all of her latest releases here:
www.christybarritt.com/newsletter-sign-up/